Writing 14

Richard Brautigan's books:

The Galilee Hitch-Hiker
Lay the Marble Tea
The Octopus Frontier
Trout Fishing in America
A Confederate General from Big Sur
In Watermelon Sugar
The Abortion
All Watched Over By Machines of Loving Grace
Please Plant This Book
The Pill Versus the Springhill Mine Disaster

TROUT FISHING IN AMERICA

a novel by

RICHARD BRAUTIGAN

Jonathan Cape Thirty Bedford Square London

This book was first published by Four Seasons Foundation
in its Writing series edited by Donald Allen

Nine chapters of this novel appeared in *Evergreen Review*,
three in *City Lights Journal*, and one in
The New Writing in the U.S.A.

First published in Great Britain 1970
© 1967 by Richard Brautigan

Marston Bates, *Man in Nature*, 2nd ed.,
© 1964, Prentice-Hall, Inc.
Englewood Cliffs, N.J.

Jonathan Cape Ltd, 30 Bedford Square, London, wc1

SBN 224 61849 0

Cover photograph by Erik Weber

PRINTED PHOTOLITHO IN GREAT BRITAIN
BY EBENEZER BAYLIS AND SON, LTD
THE TRINITY PRESS, WORCESTER, AND LONDON
BOUND BY G. AND J. KITCAT LTD, LONDON

For Jack Spicer and Ron Loewinsohn

CONTENTS

There are seductions that should be

in the Smithsonian Institute,

right next to The Spirit of St. Louis.

Writing 14

THE COVER FOR

TROUT FISHING IN AMERICA

The cover for <u>Trout Fishing in America</u> is a photograph taken late in the afternoon, a photograph of the Benjamin Franklin statue in San Francisco's Washington Square.
   Born 1706—Died 1790, Benjamin Franklin stands on a pedestal that looks like a house containing stone furniture. He holds some papers in one hand and his hat in the other.
   Then the statue speaks, saying in marble:

PRESENTED BY

H.D. COGSWELL

TO OUR

BOYS AND GIRLS

WHO WILL SOON

TAKE OUR PLACES

AND PASS ON.

   Around the base of the statue are four words facing the directions of this world, to the east WELCOME, to the west WELCOME, to the north WELCOME, to the south WELCOME. Just behind the statue are three poplar trees, almost leaf-less except for the top branches. The statue stands in front of the middle tree. All around the grass is wet from the rains of early February.

1

In the background is a tall cypress tree, almost dark like
a room. Adlai Stevenson spoke under the tree in 1956, before a crowd of 40,000 people.

There is a tall church across the street from the statue
with crosses, steeples, bells and a vast door that looks like
a huge mousehole, perhaps from a Tom and Jerry cartoon,
and written above the door is "Per L'Universo."

Around five o'clock in the afternoon of my cover for
<u>Trout Fishing in America</u>, people gather in the park across
the street from the church and they are hungry.

It's sandwich time for the poor.

But they cannot cross the street until the signal is given.
Then they all run across the street to the church and get
their sandwiches that are wrapped in newspaper. They go
back to the park and unwrap the newspaper and see what their
sandwiches are all about.

A friend of mine unwrapped his sandwich one afternoon
and looked inside to find just a leaf of spinach. That was all.

Was it Kafka who learned about America by reading the
autobiography of Benjamin Franklin . . .

Kafka who said, "I like the Americans because they are
healthy and optimistic."

KNOCK ON WOOD

(PART ONE)

As a child when did I first hear about trout fishing in America?
From whom? I guess it was a stepfather of mine.

Summer of 1942.

The old drunk told me about trout fishing. When he could
talk, he had a way of describing trout as if they were a precious
and intelligent metal.

Silver is not a good adjective to describe what I felt when
he told me about trout fishing.

I'd like to get it right.

Maybe trout steel. Steel made from trout. The clear
snow-filled river acting as foundry and heat.

Imagine Pittsburgh.

A steel that comes from trout, used to make buildings,
trains and tunnels.

The Andrew Carnegie of Trout!

The Reply of Trout Fishing in America:

I remember with particular amusement, people with three-
cornered hats fishing in the dawn.

KNOCK ON WOOD

(PART TWO)

One spring afternoon as a child in the strange town of Portland, I walked down to a different street corner, and saw a
row of old houses, huddled together like seals on a rock.
Then there was a long field that came sloping down off a hill.
The field was covered with green grass and bushes. On top
of the hill there was a grove of tall, dark trees. At a distance
I saw a waterfall come pouring down off the hill. It was long
and white and I could almost feel its cold spray.

There must be a creek there, I thought, and it probably
has trout in it.

Trout.

At last an opportunity to go trout fishing, to catch my first
trout, to behold Pittsburgh.

It was growing dark. I didn't have time to go and look at
the creek. I walked home past the glass whiskers of the
houses, reflecting the downward rushing waterfalls of night.

The next day I would go trout fishing for the first time. I
would get up early and eat my breakfast and go. I had heard
that it was better to go trout fishing early in the morning.
The trout were better for it. They had something extra in
the morning. I went home to prepare for trout fishing in
America. I didn't have any fishing tackle, so I had to fall
back on corny fishing tackle.

Like a joke.

Why did the chicken cross the road?

I bent a pin and tied it onto a piece of white string.

And slept.

The next morning I got up early and ate my breakfast. I
took a slice of white bread to use for bait. I planned on making doughballs from the soft center of the bread and putting
them on my vaudevillean hook.

I left the place and walked down to the different street

4

corner. How beautiful the field looked and the creek that came pouring down in a waterfall off the hill.

But as I got closer to the creek I could see that something was wrong. The creek did not act right. There was a strangeness to it. There was a thing about its motion that was wrong. Finally I got close enough to see what the trouble was.

The waterfall was just a flight of white wooden stairs leading up to a house in the trees.

I stood there for a long time, looking up and looking down, following the stairs with my eyes, having trouble believing.

Then I knocked on my creek and heard the sound of wood.

I ended up by being my own trout and eating the slice of bread myself.

The Reply of Trout Fishing in America:

There was nothing I could do. I couldn't change a flight of stairs into a creek. The boy walked back to where he came from. The same thing once happened to me. I remember mistaking an old woman for a trout stream in Vermont, and I had to beg her pardon.

"Excuse me," I said. "I thought you were a trout stream."

"I'm not," she said.

5

RED LIP

Seventeen years later I sat down on a rock. It was under a
tree next to an old abandoned shack that had a sheriff's
notice nailed like a funeral wreath to the front door.

NO TRESPASSING

4/17 OF A HAIKU

Many rivers had flowed past those seventeen years, and
thousands of trout, and now beside the highway and the sheriff's notice flowed yet another river, the Klamath, and I was
trying to get thirty-five miles downstream to Steelhead, the
place where I was staying.

It was all very simple. No one would stop and pick me up
even though I was carrying fishing tackle. People usually
stop and pick up a fisherman. I had to wait three hours for a
ride.

The sun was like a huge fifty-cent piece that someone had
poured kerosene on and then had lit with a match and said,
"Here, hold this while I go get a newspaper," and put the
coin in my hand, but never came back.

I had walked for miles and miles until I came to the rock
under the tree and sat down. Every time a car would come
by, about once every ten minutes, I would get up and stick
out my thumb as if it were a bunch of bananas and then sit
back down on the rock again.

The old shack had a tin roof colored reddish by years of
wear, like a hat worn under the guillotine. A corner of the
roof was loose and a hot wind blew down the river and the
loose corner clanged in the wind.

A car went by. An old couple. The car almost swerved off

the road and into the river. I guess they didn't see many
hitchhikers up there. The car went around the corner with
both of them looking back at me.

I had nothing else to do, so I caught salmon flies in my
landing net. I made up my own game. It went like this: I
couldn't chase after them. I had to let them fly to me. It
was something to do with my mind. I caught six.

A little ways up from the shack was an outhouse with its
door flung violently open. The inside of the outhouse was ex-
posed like a human face and the outhouse seemed to say,
"The old guy who built me crapped in here 9,745 times and
he's dead now and I don't want anyone else to touch me. He
was a good guy. He built me with loving care. Leave me
alone. I'm a monument now to a good ass gone under. There's
no mystery here. That's why the door's open. If you have to
crap, go in the bushes like the deer."

"Fuck you," I said to the outhouse. "All I want is a ride
down the river."

THE KOOL-AID WINO

When I was a child I had a friend who became a Kool-Aid
wino as the result of a rupture. He was a member of a very
large and poor German family. All the older children in the
family had to work in the fields during the summer, picking
beans for two-and-one-half cents a pound to keep the family
going. Everyone worked except my friend who couldn't because he was ruptured. There was no money for an opera-
tion. There wasn't even enough money to buy him a truss.
So he stayed home and became a Kool-Aid wino.

One morning in August I went over to his house. He was
still in bed. He looked up at me from underneath a tattered
revolution of old blankets. He had never slept under a sheet
in his life.

"Did you bring the nickel you promised?" he asked.

"Yeah," I said. "It's here in my pocket."

"Good."

He hopped out of bed and he was already dressed. He had
told me once that he never took off his clothes when he went
to bed.

"Why bother?" he had said. "You're only going to get up,
anyway. Be prepared for it. You're not fooling anyone by
taking your clothes off when you go to bed."

He went into the kitchen, stepping around the littlest
children, whose wet diapers were in various stages of an-
archy. He made his breakfast: a slice of homemade bread
covered with Karo syrup and peanut butter.

"Let's go," he said.

We left the house with him still eating the sandwich. The
store was three blocks away, on the other side of a field
covered with heavy yellow grass. There were many pheasants in the field. Fat with summer they barely flew away
when we came up to them.

8

"Hello," said the grocer. He was bald with a red birthmark on his head. The birthmark looked just like an old car parked on his head. He automatically reached for a package of grape Kool-Aid and put it on the counter.

"Five cents."

"He's got it," my friend said.

I reached into my pocket and gave the nickel to the grocer. He nodded and the old red car wobbled back and forth on the road as if the driver were having an epileptic seizure.

We left.

My friend led the way across the field. One of the pheasants didn't even bother to fly. He ran across the field in front of us like a feathered pig.

When we got back to my friend's house the ceremony began. To him the making of Kool-Aid was a romance and a ceremony. It had to be performed in an exact manner and with dignity.

First he got a gallon jar and we went around to the side of the house where the water spigot thrust itself out of the ground like the finger of a saint, surrounded by a mud puddle.

He opened the Kool-Aid and dumped it into the jar. Putting the jar under the spigot, he turned the water on. The water spit, splashed and guzzled out of the spigot.

He was careful to see that the jar did not overflow and the precious Kool-Aid spill out onto the ground. When the jar was full he turned the water off with a sudden but delicate motion like a famous brain surgeon removing a disordered portion of the imagination. Then he screwed the lid tightly onto the top of the jar and gave it a good shake.

The first part of the ceremony was over.

Like the inspired priest of an exotic cult, he had performed the first part of the ceremony well.

His mother came around the side of the house and said in a voice filled with sand and string, "When are you going to do the dishes? . . . Huh?"

"Soon," he said.

"Well, you better," she said.

When she left, it was as if she had never been there at all. The second part of the ceremony began with him carrying the jar very carefully to an abandoned chicken house in the back. "The dishes can wait," he said to me. Bertrand Russell could not have stated it better.

He opened the chicken house door and we went in. The

9

place was littered with half-rotten comic books. They were
like fruit under a tree. In the corner was an old mattress
and beside the mattress were four quart jars. He took the
gallon jar over to them, and filled them carefully not spill-
ing a drop. He screwed their caps on tightly and was now
ready for a day's drinking.

You're supposed to make only two quarts of Kool-Aid from
a package, but he always made a gallon, so his Kool-Aid
was a mere shadow of its desired potency. And you're supposed to add a cup of sugar to every package of Kool-Aid,
but he never put any sugar in his Kool-Aid because there
wasn't any sugar to put in it.

He created his own Kool-Aid reality and was able to illu-
minate himself by it.

ANOTHER METHOD
OF MAKING WALNUT CATSUP

And this is a very small cookbook for Trout Fishing in America
as if Trout Fishing in America were a rich gourmet and
Trout Fishing in America had Maria Callas for a girlfriend
and they ate together on a marble table with beautiful candles.

Compote of Apples

Take a dozen of golden pippins, pare them
nicely and take the core out with a small
penknife; put them into some water, and
let them be well scalded; then take a little
of the water with some sugar, and a few
apples which may be sliced into it, and
let the whole boil till it comes to a syrup;
then pour it over your pippins, and garnish
them with dried cherries and lemon-peel
cut fine. You must take care that your
pippins are not split.

And Maria Callas sang to Trout Fishing in America as
they ate their apples together.

A Standing Crust for Great Pies

Take a peck of flour and six pounds of butter
boiled in a gallon of water: skim it off into
the flour, and as little of the liquor as you
can. Work it up well into a paste, and then
pull it into pieces till it is cold. Then make
it up into what form you please.

And Trout Fishing in America smiled at Maria Callas as they ate their pie crust together.

A Spoonful Pudding

Take a spoonful of flour, a spoonful of cream or milk, an egg, a little nutmeg, ginger, and salt. Mix all together, and boil it in a little wooden dish half an hour. If you think proper you may add a few currants.

And Trout Fishing in America said, "The moon's coming out." And Maria Callas said, "Yes, it is."

Another Method of Making Walnut Catsup

Take green walnuts before the shell is formed, and grind them in a crab-mill, or pound them in a marble mortar. Squeeze out the juice through a coarse cloth, and put to every gallon of juice a pound of anchovies, and the same quantity of bay-salt, four ounces of Jamaica pepper, two of long and two of black pepper; of mace, cloves, and ginger, each an ounce, and a stick of horseradish. Boil all together till reduced to half the quantity, and then put it into a pot. When it is cold, bottle it close, and in three months it will be fit for use.

And Trout Fishing in America and Maria Callas poured walnut catsup on their hamburgers.

12

PROLOGUE TO GRIDER CREEK

Mooresville, Indiana, is the town that John Dillinger came from, and the town has a John Dillinger Museum. You can go in and look around.

Some towns are known as the peach capital of America or the cherry capital or the oyster capital, and there's always a festival and the photograph of a pretty girl in a bathing suit.

Mooresville, Indiana, is the John Dillinger capital of America.

Recently a man moved there with his wife, and he discovered hundreds of rats in his basement. They were huge, slow-moving child-eyed rats.

When his wife had to visit some of her relatives for a few days, the man went out and bought a .38 revolver and a lot of ammunition. Then he went down to the basement where the rats were, and he started shooting them. It didn't bother the rats at all. They acted as if it were a movie and started eating their dead companions for popcorn.

The man walked over to a rat that was busy eating a friend and placed the pistol against the rat's head. The rat did not move and continued eating away. When the hammer clicked back, the rat paused between bites and looked out of the corner of its eye. First at the pistol and then at the man. It was a kind of friendly look as if to say, "When my mother was young she sang like Deanna Durbin."

The man pulled the trigger.

He had no sense of humor.

There's always a single feature, a double feature and an eternal feature playing at the Great Theater in Mooresville, Indiana: the John Dillinger capital of America.

GRIDER CREEK

I had heard there was some good fishing in there and it was
running clear while all the other large creeks were running
muddy from the snow melting off the Marble Mountains.

I also heard there were some Eastern brook trout in there,
high up in the mountains, living in the wakes of beaver dams.

The guy who drove the school bus drew a map of Grider
Creek, showing where the good fishing was. We were standing in front of Steelhead Lodge when he drew the map. It was
a very hot day. I'd imagine it was a hundred degrees.

You had to have a car to get to Grider Creek where the
good fishing was, and I didn't have a car. The map was nice,
though. Drawn with a heavy dull pencil on a piece of paper
bag. With a little square ☐ for a sawmill.

14

THE BALLET FOR

TROUT FISHING IN AMERICA

How the Cobra Lily traps insects is a ballet for Trout Fishing in America, a ballet to be performed at the University of California at Los Angeles.

The plant is beside me here on the back porch.

It died a few days after I bought it at Woolworth's. That was months ago, during the presidential election of nineteen hundred and sixty.

I buried the plant in an empty Metrecal can.

The side of the can says, "Metrecal Dietary for Weight Control," and below that reads, "Ingredients: Non-fat milk solids, soya flour, whole milk solids, sucrose, starch, corn oil, coconut oil, yeast, imitation vanilla," but the can's only a graveyard now for a Cobra Lily that has turned dry and brown and has black freckles.

As a kind of funeral wreath, there is a red, white and blue button sticking in the plant and the words on it say, "I'm for Nixon."

The main energy for the ballet comes from a description of the Cobra Lily. The description could be used as a welcome mat on the front porch of hell or to conduct an orchestra of mortuaries with ice-cold woodwinds or be an atomic mailman in the pines, in the pines where the sun never shines.

"Nature has endowed the Cobra Lily with the means of catching its own food. The forked tongue is covered with honey glands which attract the insects upon which it feeds. Once inside the hood, downward pointing hairs prevent the insect from crawling out. The digestive liquids are found in the base of the plant.

"The supposition that it is necessary to feed the Cobra Lily a piece of hamburger or an insect daily is erroneous."

I hope the dancers do a good job of it, they hold our

15

imagination in their feet, dancing in Los Angeles for Trout
Fishing in America.

A WALDEN POND FOR WINOS

The autumn carried along with it, like the roller coaster of a flesh-eating plant, port wine and the people who drank that dark sweet wine, people long since gone, except for me.

Always wary of the police, we drank in the safest place we could find, the park across from the church.

There were three poplar trees in the middle of the park and there was a statue of Benjamin Franklin in front of the trees. We sat there and drank port.

At home my wife was pregnant.

I would call on the telephone after I finished work and say, "I won't be home for a little while. I'm going to have a drink with some friends."

The three of us huddled in the park, talking. They were both broken-down artists from New Orleans where they had drawn pictures of tourists in Pirate's Alley.

Now in San Francisco, with the cold autumn wind upon them, they had decided that the future held only two directions: They were either going to open up a flea circus or commit themselves to an insane asylum.

So they talked about it while they drank wine.

They talked about how to make little clothes for fleas by pasting pieces of colored paper on their backs.

They said the way that you trained fleas was to make them dependent upon you for their food. This was done by letting them feed off you at an appointed hour.

They talked about making little flea wheelbarrows and pool tables and bicycles.

They would charge fifty-cents admission for their flea circus. The business was certain to have a future to it. Perhaps they would even get on the Ed Sullivan Show.

They of course did not have their fleas yet, but they could easily be obtained from a white cat.

Then they decided that the fleas that lived on Siamese cats would probably be more intelligent than the fleas that lived on just ordinary alley cats. It only made sense that drinking intelligent blood would make intelligent fleas.

And so it went on until it was exhausted and we went and bought another fifth of port wine and returned to the trees and Benjamin Franklin.

Now it was close to sunset and the earth was beginning to cool off in the correct manner of eternity and office girls were returning like penguins from Montgomery Street. They looked at us hurriedly and mentally registered: winos.

Then the two artists talked about committing themselves to an insane asylum for the winter. They talked about how warm it would be in the insane asylum, with television, clean sheets on soft beds, hamburger gravy over mashed potatoes, a dance once a week with the lady kooks, clean clothes, a locked razor and lovely young student nurses.

Ah, yes, there was a future in the insane asylum. No winter spent there could be a total loss.

TOM MARTIN CREEK

I walked down one morning from Steelhead, following the
Klamath River that was high and murky and had the intelli-
gence of a dinosaur. Tom Martin Creek was a small creek
with cold, clear water and poured out of a canyon and
through a culvert under the highway and then into the Klamath.

I dropped a fly in a small pool just below where the creek
flowed out of the culvert and took a nine-inch trout. It was
a good-looking fish and fought all over the top of the pool.

Even though the creek was very small and poured out of
a steep brushy canyon filled with poison oak, I decided to
follow the creek up a ways because I liked the feel and motion
of the creek.

I liked the name, too.

Tom Martin Creek.

It's good to name creeks after people and then later to follow them for a while seeing what they have to offer, what
they know and have made of themselves.

But that creek turned out to be a real son-of-a-bitch. I
had to fight it all the God-damn way: brush, poison oak and
hardly any good places to fish, and sometimes the canyon
was so narrow the creek poured out like water from a faucet.
Sometimes it was so bad that it just left me standing there,
not knowing which way to jump.

You had to be a plumber to fish that creek.

After that first trout I was alone in there. But I didn't
know it until later.

TROUT FISHING ON THE BEVEL

The two graveyards were next to each other on small hills and between them flowed Graveyard Creek, a slow-moving, funeral-procession-on-a-hot-day creek with a lot of fine trout in it.

And the dead didn't mind me fishing there at all.

One graveyard had tall fir trees growing in it, and the grass was kept Peter Pan green all year round by pumping water up from the creek, and the graveyard had fine marble headstones and statues and tombs.

The other graveyard was for the poor and it had no trees and the grass turned a flat-tire brown in the summer and stayed that way until the rain, like a mechanic, began in the late autumn.

There were no fancy headstones for the poor dead. Their markers were small boards that looked like heels of stale bread:

Devoted Slob Father Of

Beloved Worked-to-Death Mother Of

On some of the graves were fruit jars and tin cans with wilted flowers in them:

Sacred

To the Memory

of

John Talbot

Who at the Age of Eighteen

Had His Ass Shot Off

In a Honky-Tonk

November 1, 1936

This Mayonnaise Jar

With Wilted Flowers In It

Was Left Here Six Months Ago

By His Sister

Who Is In

The Crazy Place Now.

Eventually the seasons would take care of their wooden
names like a sleepy short-order cook cracking eggs over a
grill next to a railroad station. Whereas the well-to-do
would have their names for a long time written on marble
hors d'oeuvres like horses trotting up the fancy paths to the
sky.

I fished Graveyard Creek in the dusk when the hatch was
on and worked some good trout out of there. Only the pover-
ty of the dead bothered me.

Once, while cleaning the trout before I went home in the
almost night, I had a vision of going over to the poor graveyard and gathering up grass and fruit jars and tin cans and
markers and wilted flowers and bugs and weeds and clods
and going home and putting a hook in the vise and tying a fly
with all that stuff and then going outside and casting it up
into the sky, watching it float over clouds and then into the
evening star.

21

SEA, SEA RIDER

The man who owned the bookstore was not magic. He was not a
three-legged crow on the dandelion side of the mountain.

He was, of course, a Jew, a retired merchant seaman
who had been torpedoed in the North Atlantic and floated
there day after day until death did not want him. He had a
young wife, a heart attack, a Volkswagen and a home in
Marin County. He liked the works of George Orwell, Richard
Aldington and Edmund Wilson.

He learned about life at sixteen, first from Dostoevsky
and then from the whores of New Orleans.

The bookstore was a parking lot for used graveyards.
Thousands of graveyards were parked in rows like cars.
Most of the books were out of print, and no one wanted to
read them any more and the people who had read the books
had died or forgotten about them, but through the organic
process of music the books had become virgins again. They
wore their ancient copyrights like new maidenheads.

I went to the bookstore in the afternoons after I got off
work, during that terrible year of 1959.

He had a kitchen in the back of the store and he brewed
cups of thick Turkish coffee in a copper pan. I drank coffee
and read old books and waited for the year to end. He had a
small room above the kitchen.

It looked down on the bookstore and had Chinese screens
in front of it. The room contained a couch, a glass cabinet
with Chinese things in it and a table and three chairs. There
was a tiny bathroom fastened like a watch fob to the room.

I was sitting on a stool in the bookstore one afternoon
reading a book that was in the shape of a chalice. The book
had clear pages like gin, and the first page in the book read:

Billy

the Kid

born

November 23,

1859

in

New York

City

The owner of the bookstore came up to me, and put his
arm on my shoulder and said, "Would you like to get laid?"
His voice was very kind.

"No," I said.

"You're wrong," he said, and then without saying anything
else, he went out in front of the bookstore, and stopped a pair
of total strangers, a man and a woman. He talked to them for
a few moments. I couldn't hear what he was saying. He pointed at me in the bookstore. The woman nodded her head and
then the man nodded his head.

They came into the bookstore.

I was embarrassed. I could not leave the bookstore because they were entering by the only door, so I decided to
go upstairs and go to the toilet. I got up abruptly and walked
to the back of the bookstore and went upstairs to the bathroom, and they followed after me.

I could hear them on the stairs.

I waited for a long time in the bathroom and they waited
an equally long time in the other room. They never spoke.
When I came out of the bathroom, the woman was lying naked
on the couch, and the man was sitting in a chair with his hat
on his lap.

"Don't worry about him," the girl said. "These things
make no difference to him. He's rich. He has 3,859 Rolls
Royces." The girl was very pretty and her body was like a
clear mountain river of skin and muscle flowing over rocks
of bone and hidden nerves.

"Come to me," she said. "And come inside me for we are Aquarius and I love you."

I looked at the man sitting in the chair. He was not smiling and he did not look sad.

I took off my shoes and all my clothes. The man did not say a word.

The girl's body moved ever so slightly from side to side.

There was nothing else I could do for my body was like birds sitting on a telephone wire strung out down the world, clouds tossing the wires carefully.

I laid the girl.

It was like the eternal 59th second when it becomes a minute and then looks kind of sheepish.

"Good," the girl said, and kissed me on the face.

The man sat there without speaking or moving or sending out any emotion into the room. I guess he <u>was</u> rich and owned 3,859 Rolls Royces.

Afterwards the girl got dressed and she and the man left. They walked down the stairs and on their way out, I heard him say his first words.

"Would you like to go to Ernie's for dinner?"

"I don't know," the girl said. "It's a little early to think about dinner."

Then I heard the door close and they were gone. I got dressed and went downstairs. The flesh about my body felt soft and relaxed like an experiment in functional background music.

The owner of the bookstore was sitting at his desk behind the counter. "I'll tell you what happened up there," he said, in a beautiful anti-three-legged-crow voice, in an anti-dandelion side of the mountain voice.

"What?" I said.

"You fought in the Spanish Civil War. You were a young Communist from Cleveland, Ohio. She was a painter. A New York Jew who was sightseeing in the Spanish Civil War as if it were the Mardi Gras in New Orleans being acted out by Greek statues.

"She was drawing a picture of a dead anarchist when you met her. She asked you to stand beside the anarchist and act as if you had killed him. You slapped her across the face and said something that would be embarrassing for me to repeat.

24

"You both fell very much in love.

"Once while you were at the front she read Anatomy of Melancholy and did 349 drawings of a lemon.

"Your love for each other was mostly spiritual. Neither one of you performed like millionaires in bed.

"When Barcelona fell, you and she flew to England, and then took a ship back to New York. Your love for each other remained in Spain. It was only a war love. You loved only yourselves, loving each other in Spain during the war. On the Atlantic you were different toward each other and became every day more and more like people lost from each other.

"Every wave on the Atlantic was like a dead seagull dragging its driftwood artillery from horizon to horizon.

"When the ship bumped up against America, you departed without saying anything and never saw each other again. The last I heard of you, you were still living in Philadelphia."

"That's what you think happened up there?" I said.

"Partly," he said. "Yes, that's part of it."

He took out his pipe and filled it with tobacco and lit it.

"Do you want me to tell you what else happened up there?" he said.

"Go ahead."

"You crossed the border into Mexico," he said. "You rode your horse into a small town. The people knew who you were and they were afraid of you. They knew you had killed many men with that gun you wore at your side. The town itself was so small that it didn't have a priest.

"When the rurales saw you, they left the town. Tough as they were, they did not want to have anything to do with you. The rurales left.

"You became the most powerful man in town.

"You were seduced by a thirteen-year-old girl, and you and she lived together in an adobe hut, and practically all you did was make love

"She was slender and had long dark hair. You made love standing, sitting, lying on the dirt floor with pigs and chickens around you. The walls, the floor and even the roof of the hut were coated with your sperm and her come.

"You slept on the floor at night and used your sperm for a pillow and her come for a blanket.

"The people in the town were so afraid of you that they could do nothing.

"After a while she started going around town without any clothes on, and the people of the town said that it was not a good thing, and when you started going around without any clothes, and when both of you began making love on the back of your horse in the middle of the zocalo, the people of the town became so afraid that they abandoned the town. It's been abandoned ever since.

"People won't live there.

"Neither of you lived to be twenty-one. It was not necessary.

"See, I do know what happened upstairs," he said. He smiled at me kindly. His eyes were like the shoelaces of a harpsichord.

I thought about what happened upstairs.

"You know what I say is the truth," he said. "For you saw it with your own eyes and traveled it with your own body. Finish the book you were reading before you were interrupted. I'm glad you got laid."

Once resumed, the pages of the book began to speed up and turn faster and faster until they were spinning like wheels in the sea.

THE LAST YEAR THE TROUT
CAME UP HAYMAN CREEK

Gone now the old fart. Hayman Creek was named for
Charles Hayman, a sort of half-assed pioneer in a country
that not many wanted to live in because it was poor and ugly
and horrible. He built a shack, this was in 1876, on a little
creek that drained a worthless hill. After a while the creek
was called Hayman Creek.

Mr. Hayman did not know how to read or write and considered himself better for it. Mr. Hayman did odd jobs for
years and years and years and years.

Your mule's broke?

Get Mr. Hayman to fix it.

Your fences are on fire?

Get Mr. Hayman to put them out.

Mr. Hayman lived on a diet of stone-ground wheat and
kale. He bought the wheat by the hundred-pound sack and
ground it himself with a mortar and pestle. He grew the kale
in front of his shack and tended the kale as if it were prize-
winning orchids.

During all the time that was his life, Mr. Hayman never
had a cup of coffee, a smoke, a drink or a woman and thought
he'd be a fool if he did.

In the winter a few trout would go up Hayman Creek, but
by early summer the creek was almost dry and there were
no fish in it.

Mr. Hayman used to catch a trout or two and eat raw
trout with his stone-ground wheat and his kale, and then one
day he was so old that he did not feel like working any more,
and he looked so old that the children thought he must be evil
to live by himself, and they were afraid to go up the creek
near his shack.

It didn't bother Mr. Hayman. The last thing in the world
he had any use for were children. Reading and writing and

27

children were all the same, Mr. Hayman thought, and ground his wheat and tended his kale and caught a trout or two when they were in the creek.

He looked ninety years old for thirty years and then he got the notion that he would die, and did so. The year he died the trout didn't come up Hayman Creek, and never went up the creek again. With the old man dead, the trout figured it was better to stay where they were.

The mortar and pestle fell off the shelf and broke.

The shack rotted away.

And the weeds grew into the kale.

Twenty years after Mr. Hayman's death, some fish and game people were planting trout in the streams around there.

"Might as well put some here," one of the men said.

"Sure," the other one said.

They dumped a can full of trout in the creek and no sooner had the trout touched the water, than they turned their white bellies up and floated dead down the creek.

TROUT DEATH BY PORT WINE

It was not an outhouse resting upon the imagination.

It was reality.

An eleven-inch rainbow trout was killed. Its life taken forever from the waters of the earth, by giving it a drink of port wine.

It is against the natural order of death for a trout to die by having a drink of port wine.

It is all right for a trout to have its neck broken by a fisherman and then to be tossed into the creel or for a trout to die from a fungus that crawls like sugar-colored ants over its body until the trout is in death's sugarbowl.

It is all right for a trout to be trapped in a pool that dries up in the late summer or to be caught in the talons of a bird or the claws of an animal.

Yes, it is even all right for a trout to be killed by pollution, to die in a river of suffocating human excrement.

There are trout that die of old age and their white beards flow to the sea.

All these things are in the natural order of death, but for a trout to die from a drink of port wine, that is another thing.

No mention of it in "The treatyse of fysshynge wyth an angle," in the Boke of St. Albans, published 1496. No mention of it in Minor Tactics of the Chalk Stream, by H. C. Cutcliffe, published in 1910. No mention of it in Truth Is Stranger than Fishin', by Beatrice Cook, published in 1955. No mention of it in Northern Memoirs, by Richard Franck, published in 1694. No mention of it in I Go A-Fishing, by W. C. Prime, published in 1873. No mention of it in Trout Fishing and Trout Flies, by Jim Quick, published in 1957. No mention of it in Certaine Experiments Concerning Fish and Fruite, by John Taverner, published in 1600. No mention of it in A River Never Sleeps, by Roderick L. Haig Brown, published

29

in 1946. No mention of it in <u>Till Fish Us Do Part</u>, by Beatrice
Cook, published in 1949. No mention of it in <u>The Flyfisher &</u>
<u>the Trout's Point of View</u>, by Col. E. W. Harding, published
in 1931. No mention of it in <u>Chalk Stream Studies</u>, by Charles
Kingsley, published in 1859. No mention of it in <u>Trout Mad-</u>
<u>ness</u>, by Robert Traver, published in 1960.
 No mention of it in <u>Sunshine and the Dry Fly</u>, by J. W.
Dunne, published in 1924. No mention of it in <u>Just Fishing</u>,
by Ray Bergman, published in 1932. No mention of it in
<u>Matching the Hatch</u>, by Ernest G. Schwiebert, Jr., pub-
lished in 1955. No mention of it in <u>The Art of Trout Fishing</u>
<u>on Rapid Streams</u>, by H. C. Cutcliffe, published in 1863. No
mention of it in <u>Old Flies in New Dresses</u>, by C. E. Walker,
published in 1898. No mention of it in <u>Fisherman's Spring</u>,
by Roderick L. Haig-Brown, published in 1951. No mention
of it in <u>The Determined Angler and the Brook Trout</u>, by
Charles Bradford, published in 1916. No mention of it in
<u>Women Can Fish</u>, by Chisie Farrington, published in 1951.
No mention of it in <u>Tales of the Angler's El Dorado New Zea-</u>
<u>land</u>, by Zane Grey, published in 1926. No mention of it in
<u>The Flyfisher's Guide</u>, by G. C. Bainbridge, published in
1816.
 There's no mention of a trout dying by having a drink of
port wine anywhere.

 To describe the Supreme Executioner: We woke up in the
morning and it was dark outside. He came kind of smiling
into the kitchen and we ate breakfast.
 Fried potatoes and eggs and coffee.
 "Well, you old bastard," he said. "Pass the salt."
 The tackle was already in the car, so we just got in and
drove away. Beginning at the first light of dawn, we hit the
road at the bottom of the mountains, and drove up into the
dawn.
 The light behind the trees was like going into a gradual
and strange department store.
 "That was a good-looking girl last night," he said.
 "Yeah," I said. "You did all right."
 "If the shoe fits . . ." he said.
 Owl Snuff Creek was just a small creek, only a few miles
long, but there were some nice trout in it. We got out of the
car and walked a quarter of a mile down the mountainside to

the creek. I put my tackle together. He pulled a pint of port wine out of his jacket pocket and said, "Wouldn't you know."

"No thanks," I said.

He took a good snort and then shook his head, side to side, and said, "Do you know what this creek reminds me of?"

"No," I said, tying a gray and yellow fly onto my leader.

"It reminds me of Evangeline's vagina, a constant dream of my childhood and promoter of my youth."

"That's nice," I said.

"Longfellow was the Henry Miller of my childhood," he said.

"Good," I said.

I cast into a little pool that had a swirl of fir needles going around the edge of it. The fir needles went around and around. It made no sense that they should come from trees. They looked perfectly contented and natural in the pool as if the pool had grown them on watery branches.

I had a good hit on my third cast, but missed it.

"Oh, boy," he said. "I think I'll watch you fish. The stolen painting is in the house next door."

I fished upstream coming ever closer and closer to the narrow staircase of the canyon. Then I went up into it as if I were entering a department store. I caught three trout in the lost and found department. He didn't even put his tackle together. He just followed after me, drinking port wine and poking a stick at the world.

"This is a beautiful creek," he said. "It reminds me of Evangeline's hearing aid."

We ended up at a large pool that was formed by the creek crashing through the children's toy section. At the beginning of the pool the water was like cream, then it mirrored out and reflected the shadow of a large tree. By this time the sun was up. You could see it coming down the mountain.

I cast into the cream and let my fly drift down onto a long branch of the tree, next to a bird.

Go-wham!

I set the hook and the trout started jumping.

"Giraffe races at Kilimanjaro!" he shouted, and every time the trout jumped, he jumped.

"Bee races at Mount Everest!" he shouted.

I didn't have a net with me so I fought the trout over to the edge of the creek and swung it up onto the shore.

31

The trout had a big red stripe down its side.

It was a good rainbow.

"What a beauty," he said.

He picked it up and it was squirming in his hands.

"Break its neck," I said.

"I have a better idea," he said. "Before I kill it, let me at least soothe its approach into death. This trout needs a drink." He took the bottle of port out of his pocket, unscrewed the cap and poured a good slug into the trout's mouth.

The trout went into a spasm.

Its body shook very rapidly like a telescope during an earthquake. The mouth was wide open and chattering almost as if it had human teeth.

He laid the trout on a white rock, head down, and some of the wine trickled out of its mouth and made a stain on the rock.

The trout was lying very still now.

"It died happy," he said.

"This is my ode to Alcoholics Anonymous.

"Look here!"

THE AUTOPSY OF

TROUT FISHING IN AMERICA

This is the autopsy of Trout Fishing in America as if Trout
Fishing in America had been Lord Byron and had died in
Missolonghi, Greece, and afterward never saw the shores
of Idaho again, never saw Carrie Creek, Worsewick Hot
Springs, Paradise Creek, Salt Creek and Duck Lake again.

The Autopsy of Trout Fishing in America:

"The body was in excellent state and appeared as one that
had died suddenly of asphyxiation. The bony cranial vault
was opened and the bones of the cranium were found very
hard without any traces of the sutures like the bones of a
person 80 years, so much so that one would have said that
the cranium was formed by one solitary bone. . . . The
meninges were attached to the internal walls of the cranium
so firmly that while sawing the bone around the interior to
detach the bone from the dura the strength of two robust men
was not sufficient. . . . The cerebrum with cerebellum
weighed about six medical pounds. The kidneys were very
large but healthy and the urinary bladder was relatively
small."

On May 2, 1824, the body of Trout Fishing in America
left Missolonghi by ship destined to arrive in England on the
evening of June 29, 1824.

Trout Fishing in America's body was preserved in a cask
holding one hundred-eighty gallons of spirits: O, a long way
from Idaho, a long way from Stanley Basin, Little Redfish
Lake, the Big Lost River and from Lake Josephus and the
Big Wood River.

33

THE MESSAGE

Last night a blue thing, the smoke itself, from our campfire
drifted down the valley, entering into the sound of the bell-
mare until the blue thing and the bell could not be separated,
no matter how hard you tried. There was no crowbar big
enough to do the job.

Yesterday afternoon we drove down the road from Wells
Summit, then we ran into the sheep. They also were being
moved on the road.

A shepherd walked in front of the car, a leafy branch in
his hand, sweeping the sheep aside. He looked like a young,
skinny Adolf Hitler, but friendly.

I guess there were a thousand sheep on the road. It was
hot and dusty and noisy and took what seemed like a long
time.

At the end of the sheep was a covered wagon being pulled
by two horses. There was a third horse, the bellmare, tied
on the back of the wagon. The white canvas rippled in the
wind and the wagon had no driver. The seat was empty.

Finally the Adolf Hitler, but friendly, shepherd got the
last of them out of the way. He smiled and we waved and said
thank you.

We were looking for a good place to camp. We drove down
the road, following the Little Smoky about five miles and
didn't see a place that we liked, so we decided to turn around
and go back to a place we had seen just a ways up Carrie
Creek.

"I hope those God-damn sheep aren't on the road," I said.

We drove back to where we had seen them on the road
and, of course, they were gone, but as we drove on up the
road, we just kept following sheep shit. It was ahead of us
for the next mile.

I kept looking down on the meadow by the Little Smoky, hoping to see the sheep down there, but there wasn't a sheep in sight, only the shit in front of us on the road.

As if it were a game invented by the sphincter muscle, we knew what the score was. Shaking our heads side to side, waiting.

Then we went around a bend and the sheep burst like a roman candle all over the road and again a thousand sheep and the shepherd in front of us, wondering what the fuck. The same thing was in our minds.

There was some beer in the back seat. It wasn't exactly cold, but it wasn't warm either. I tell you I was really embarrassed. I took a bottle of beer and got out of the car.

I walked up to the shepherd who looked like Adolf Hitler, but friendly.

"I'm sorry," I said.

"It's the sheep," he said. (O sweet and distant blossoms of Munich and Berlin!) "Sometimes they are a trouble but it all works out."

"Would you like a bottle of beer?" I said. "I'm sorry to put you through this again."

"Thank you," he said, shrugging his shoulders. He took the beer over and put it on the empty seat of the wagon. That's how it looked. After a long time, we were free of the sheep. They were like a net dragged finally away from the car.

We drove up to the place on Carrie Creek and pitched the tent and took our goods out of the car and piled them in the tent.

Then we drove up the creek a ways, above the place where there were beaver dams and the trout stared back at us like fallen leaves.

We filled the back of the car with wood for the fire and I caught a mess of those leaves for dinner. They were small and dark and cold. The autumn was good to us.

When we got back to our camp, I saw the shepherd's wagon down the road a ways and on the meadow I heard the bell-mare and the very distant sound of the sheep.

It was the final circle with the Adolf Hitler, but friendly, shepherd as the diameter. He was camping down there for the night. So in the dusk, the blue smoke from our campfire went down and got in there with the bellmare.

35

The sheep lulled themselves into senseless sleep, one following another like the banners of a lost army. I have here a very important message that just arrived a few moments ago. It says "Stalingrad."

TROUT FISHING IN AMERICA

TERRORISTS

> Long live our friend the revolver!
> Long live our friend the machine-gun!
>
> —Israeli terrorist chant

One April morning in the sixth grade, we became, first by
accident and then by premeditation, trout fishing in America
terrorists.

It came about this way: we were a strange bunch of kids.

We were always being called in before the principal for
daring and mischievous deeds. The principal was a young
man and a genius in the way he handled us.

One April morning we were standing around in the play
yard, acting as if it were a huge open-air poolhall with the
first-graders coming and going like pool balls. We were all
bored with the prospect of another day's school, studying
Cuba.

One of us had a piece of white chalk and as a first-grader
went walking by, the one of us absentmindedly wrote "Trout
fishing in America" on the back of the first-grader.

The first-grader strained around, trying to read what was
written on his back, but he couldn't see what it was, so he
shrugged his shoulders and went off to play on the swings.

We watched the first-grader walk away with "Trout fishing in America" written on his back. It looked good and
seemed quite natural and pleasing to the eye that a first-
grader should have "Trout fishing in America" written in
chalk on his back.

The next time I saw a first-grader, I borrowed my friend's
piece of chalk and said, "First-grader, you're wanted over
here."

37

The first-grader came over to me and I said, "Turn around."

The first-grader turned around and I wrote "Trout fishing in America" on his back. It looked even better on the second first-grader. We couldn't help but admire it. "Trout fishing in America." It certainly did add something to the first-graders. It completed them and gave them a kind of class.

"It really looks good, doesn't it?"

"Yeah."

"Let's get some more chalk."

"Sure."

"There are a lot of first-graders over there by the monkeybars."

"Yeah."

We all got hold of chalk and later in the day, by the end of lunch period, almost all of the first-graders had "Trout fishing in America" written on their backs, girls included.

Complaints began arriving at the principal's office from the first-grade teachers. One of the complaints was in the form of a little girl.

"Miss Robins sent me," she said to the principal. "She told me to have you look at this."

"Look at what?" the principal said, staring at the empty child.

"At my back," she said.

The little girl turned around and the principal read aloud, "Trout fishing in America."

"Who did this?" the principal said.

"That gang of sixth-graders," she said. "The bad ones. They've done it to all us first-graders. We all look like this. 'Trout fishing in America.' What does it mean? I just got this sweater new from my grandma."

"Huh. 'Trout fishing in America,'" the principal said."Tell Miss Robins I'll be down to see her in a little while," and excused the girl and a short time later we terrorists were summoned up from the lower world.

We reluctantly stamped into the principal's office, fidgeting and pawing our feet and looking out the windows and yawning and one of us suddenly got an insane blink going and putting our hands into our pockets and looking away and then back again and looking up at the light fixture on the ceiling, how much it looked like a boiled potato, and down again and at the

38

picture of the principal's mother on the wall. She had been a
star in the silent pictures and was tied to a railroad track.

"Does 'Trout fishing in America' seem at all familiar to
you boys?" the principal said. "I wonder if perhaps you've
seen it written down anywhere today in your travels? 'Trout
fishing in America.' Think hard about it for a minute."

We all thought hard about it.

There was a silence in the room, a silence that we all
knew intimately, having been at the principal's office quite a
few times in the past.

"Let me see if I can help you," the principal said. "Perhaps you saw 'Trout fishing in America' written in chalk on
the backs of the first-graders. I wonder how it got there."

We couldn't help but smile nervously.

"I just came back from Miss Robin's first-grade class,"
the principal said. "I asked all those who had 'Trout fishing
in America' written on their backs to hold up their hands, and
all the children in the class held up their hands, except one
and he had spent his whole lunch period hiding in the lavatory.
What do you boys make of it . . . ? This 'Trout fishing in
America' business?"

We didn't say anything.

The one of us still had his mad blink going. I am certain
that it was his guilty blink that always gave us away. We
should have gotten rid of him at the beginning of the sixth
grade.

"You're all guilty, aren't you?" he said. "Is there one of
you who isn't guilty? If there is, speak up. Now."

We were all silent except for blink, blink, blink, blink, blink.
Suddenly I could <u>hear</u> his God-damn eye blinking. It was very much
like the sound of an insect laying the 1,000,000th egg of our
disaster.

"The whole bunch of you did it. Why? . . . Why 'Trout
fishing in America' on the backs of the first-graders?"

And then the principal went into his famous $E=MC^2$ sixth-
grade gimmick, the thing he always used in dealing with us.

"Now wouldn't it look funny," he said. "If I asked all your
teachers to come in here, and then I told the teachers all to
turn around, and then I took a piece of chalk and wrote 'Trout
fishing in America' on their backs?"

We all giggled nervously and blushed faintly.

"Would you like to see your teachers walking around all
day with 'Trout fishing in America' written on their backs,

trying to teach you about Cuba? That would look silly, wouldn't it? You wouldn't like to see that, would you? That wouldn't do at all, would it?"

"No," we said like a Greek chorus, some of us saying it with our voices and some of us by nodding our heads, and then there was the blink, blink, blink.

"That's what I thought," he said. "The first-graders look up to you and admire you like the teachers look up to me and admire me. It just won't do to write 'Trout fishing in America' on their backs. Are we agreed, gentlemen?"

We were agreed.

I tell you it worked every God-damn time.

Of course it had to work.

"All right," he said. "I'll consider trout fishing in America to have come to an end. Agreed?"

"Agreed."

"Agreed?"

"Agreed."

"Blink, blink."

But it wasn't completely over, for it took a while to get trout fishing in America off the clothes of the first-graders. A fair percentage of trout fishing in America was gone the next day. The mothers did this by simply putting clean clothes on their children, but there were a lot of kids whose mothers just tried to wipe it off and then sent them back to school the next day with the same clothes on, but you could still see "Trout fishing in America" faintly outlined on their backs. But after a few more days trout fishing in America disappeared altogether as it was destined to from its very beginning, and a kind of autumn fell over the first grade.

TROUT FISHING IN AMERICA

WITH THE FBI

Dear Trout Fishing in America,

last week walking along lower market on the way to work
saw the pictures of the FBI's TEN MOST WANTED MEN in
the window of a store. the dodger under one of the pictures
was folded under at both sides and you couldn't read all of it.
the picture showed a nice, clean-cut-looking guy with freckles
and curly (red?) hair

WANTED FOR:
RICHARD LAWRENCE MARQUETTE
Aliases: Richard Lawrence Marquette, Richard
Lourence Marquette
Description:
26, born Dec. 12, 1934, Portland, Oregon
170 to 180 pounds
muscular
light brown, cut short
blue
Complexion: ruddy
Race: white
Nationality: American
Occupations: auto body w
recapper, s
survey rod
arks: 6" hernia scar; tattoo "Mom" in wreath on
ight forearm
ull upper denture, may also have lower denture.
Reportedly frequents
s, and is an avid trout fisherman.

(this is how the dodger looked cut off on both sides and you couldn't make out any more, even what he was wanted for.)

Your old buddy,

Pard

Dear Pard,

Your letter explains why I saw two FBI agents watching a trout stream last week. They watched a path that came down through the trees and then circled a large black stump and led to a deep pool. Trout were rising in the pool. The FBI agents watched the path, the trees, the black stump, the pool and the trout as if they were all holes punched in a card that had just come out of a computer. The afternoon sun kept changing everything as it moved across the sky, and the FBI agents kept changing with the sun. It appears to be part of their training.

Your friend,

Trout Fishing in America

WORSEWICK

Worsewick Hot Springs was nothing fancy. Somebody put some boards across the creek. That was it.

The boards dammed up the creek enough to form a huge bathtub there, and the creek flowed over the top of the boards, invited like a postcard to the ocean a thousand miles away.

As I said Worsewick was nothing fancy, not like the places where the swells go. There were no buildings around. We saw an old shoe lying by the tub.

The hot springs came down off a hill and where they flowed there was a bright orange scum through the sagebrush. The hot springs flowed into the creek right there at the tub and that's where it was nice.

We parked our car on the dirt road and went down and took off our clothes, then we took off the baby's clothes, and the deerflies had at us until we got into the water, and then they stopped.

There was a green slime growing around the edges of the tub and there were dozens of dead fish floating in our bath. Their bodies had been turned white by death, like frost on iron doors. Their eyes were large and stiff.

The fish had made the mistake of going down the creek too far and ending up in hot water, singing, "When you lose your money, learn to lose."

We played and relaxed in the water. The green slime and the dead fish played and relaxed with us and flowed out over us and entwined themselves about us.

Splashing around in that hot water with my woman, I began to get ideas, as they say. After a while I placed my body in such a position in the water that the baby could not see my hard-on.

I did this by going deeper and deeper in the water, like a

dinosaur, and letting the green slime and dead fish cover me over.

My woman took the baby out of the water and gave her a bottle and put her back in the car. The baby was tired. It was <u>really</u> time for her to take a nap.

My woman took a blanket out of the car and covered up the windows that faced the hot springs. She put the blanket on top of the car and then lay rocks on the blanket to hold it in place. I remember her standing there by the car.

Then she came back to the water, and the deerflies were at her, and then it was my turn. After a while she said, "I don't have my diaphragm with me and besides it wouldn't work in the water, anyway. I think it's a good idea if you don't come inside me. What do you think?"

I thought this over and said all right. I didn't want any more kids for a long time. The green slime and dead fish were all about our bodies.

I remember a dead fish floated under her neck. I waited for it to come up on the other side, and it came up on the other side.

Worsewick was nothing fancy.

Then I came, and just cleared her in a split second like an airplane in the movies, pulling out of a nosedive and sailing over the roof of a school.

My sperm came out into the water, unaccustomed to the light, and instantly it became a misty, stringy kind of thing and swirled out like a falling star, and I saw a dead fish come forward and float into my sperm, bending it in the middle. His eyes were stiff like iron.

THE SHIPPING OF TROUT
FISHING IN AMERICA SHORTY
TO NELSON ALGREN

Trout Fishing in America Shorty appeared suddenly last
autumn in San Francisco, staggering around in a magnificent
chrome-plated steel wheelchair.

He was a legless, screaming middle-aged wino.

He descended upon North Beach like a chapter from the
Old Testament. He was the reason birds migrate in the
autumn. They have to. He was the cold turning of the earth;
the bad wind that blows off sugar.

He would stop children on the street and say to them, "I
ain't got no legs. The trout chopped my legs off in Fort
Lauderdale. You kids got legs. The trout didn't chop your
legs off. Wheel me into that store over there."

The kids, frightened and embarrassed, would wheel Trout
Fishing in America Shorty into the store. It would always be
a store that sold sweet wine, and he would buy a bottle of
wine and then he'd have the kids wheel him back out onto the
street, and he would open the wine and start drinking there
on the street just like he was Winston Churchill.

After a while the children would run and hide when they
saw Trout Fishing in America Shorty coming.

"I pushed him last week,"

"I pushed him yesterday,"

"Quick, let's hide behind these garbage cans."

And they would hide behind the garbage cans while Trout
Fishing in America Shorty staggered by in his wheelchair.
The kids would hold their breath until he was gone.

Trout Fishing in America Shorty used to go down to
L'Italia, the Italian newspaper in North Beach at Stockton
and Green Streets. Old Italians gather in front of the newspaper in the afternoon and just stand there, leaning up
against the building, talking and dying in the sun.

45

Trout Fishing in America Shorty used to wheel into the
middle of them as if they were a bunch of pigeons, bottle of
wine in hand, and begin shouting obscenities in fake Italian.

Tra-la-la-la-la-la-Spa-ghet-tiii!

I remember Trout Fishing in America Shorty passed out
in Washington Square, right in front of the Benjamin Franklin statue. He had fallen face first out of his wheelchair and
just lay there without moving.

Snoring loudly.

Above him were the metal works of Benjamin Franklin
like a clock, hat in hand.

Trout Fishing in America Shorty lay there below, his
face spread out like a fan in the grass.

A friend and I got to talking about Trout Fishing in America Shorty one afternoon. We decided the best thing to do with
him was to pack him in a big shipping crate with a couple of
cases of sweet wine and send him to Nelson Algren.

Nelson Algren is always writing about Railroad Shorty, a
hero of the Neon Wilderness (the reason for "The Face on
the Barroom Floor") and the destroyer of Dove Linkhorn in
A Walk on the Wild Side.

We thought that Nelson Algren would make the perfect
custodian for Trout Fishing in America Shorty. Maybe a
museum might be started. Trout Fishing in America Shorty
could be the first piece in an important collection.

We would nail him up in a packing crate with a big label
on it.

> Contents:
> Trout Fishing in America Shorty
>
> Occupation:
> Wino
>
> Address:
> C/O Nelson Algren
> Chicago

And there would be stickers all over the crate, saying:
"GLASS/HANDLE WITH CARE/SPECIAL HANDLING/GLASS
/DON'T SPILL/THIS SIDE UP/HANDLE THIS WINO LIKE HE
WAS AN ANGEL"

And Trout Fishing in America Shorty, grumbling, puking
and cursing in his crate would travel across America, from
San Francisco to Chicago.

And Trout Fishing in America Shorty, wondering what it was all about, would travel on, shouting, "Where in the hell am I? I can't see to open this bottle! Who turned out the lights? Fuck this motel! I have to take a piss! Where's my key?"

It was a good idea.

A few days after we made our plans for Trout Fishing in America Shorty, a heavy rain was pouring down upon San Francisco. The rain turned the streets inward, like drowned lungs, upon themselves and I was hurrying to work, meeting swollen gutters at the intersections.

I saw Trout Fishing in America Shorty passed out in the front window of a Filipino laundromat. He was sitting in his wheelchair with closed eyes staring out the window.

There was a tranquil expression on his face. He almost looked human. He had probably fallen asleep while he was having his brains washed in one of the machines.

Weeks passed and we never got around to shipping Trout Fishing in America Shorty away to Nelson Algren. We kept putting it off. One thing and another. Then we lost our golden opportunity because Trout Fishing in America Shorty disappeared a little while after that.

They probably swept him up one morning and put him in jail to punish him, the evil fart, or they put him in a nuthouse to dry him out a little.

Maybe Trout Fishing in America Shorty just pedaled down to San Jose in his wheelchair, rattling along the freeway at a quarter of a mile an hour.

I don't know what happened to him. But if he comes back to San Francisco someday and dies, I have an idea.

Trout Fishing in America Shorty should be buried right beside the Benjamin Franklin statue in Washington Square. We should anchor his wheelchair to a huge gray stone and write upon the stone:

Trout Fishing in America Shorty
20¢ Wash
10¢ Dry
Forever

47

THE MAYOR

OF THE TWENTIETH CENTURY

London. On December 1, 1887; July 7, August 8, September
30, one day in the month of October and on the 9th of November, 1888; on the 1st of June, the 17th of July and the 10th
of September 1889 . . .

The disguise was perfect.

Nobody ever saw him, except, of course, the victims.
They saw him.

Who would have expected?

He wore a costume of trout fishing in America. He wore
mountains on his elbows and bluejays on the collar of his
shirt. Deep water flowed through the lilies that were entwined
about his shoelaces. A bullfrog kept croaking in his watch
pocket and the air was filled with the sweet smell of ripe
blackberry bushes.

He wore trout fishing in America as a costume to hide
his own appearance from the world while he performed his
deeds of murder in the night.

Who would have expected?

Nobody!

Scotland Yard?

(Pouf!)

They were always a hundred miles away, wearing halibut-
stalker hats, looking under the dust.

Nobody ever found out.

O, now he's the Mayor of the Twentieth Century! A razor,
a knife and a ukelele are his favorite instruments.

Of course, it would have to be a ukelele. Nobody else
would have thought of it, pulled like a plow through the intestines.

ON PARADISE

"Speaking of evacuations, your missive, while complete in other regards, skirted the subject, though you did deal briefly with rural micturition procedure. I consider this a gross oversight on your part, as I'm certain you're well aware of my unending fascination with camp-out crapping. Please rush details in your next effort. Slit-trench, pith helmet, slingshot, biffy and if so number of holes and proximity of keester to vermin and deposits of prior users."

—From a Letter by a Friend

Sheep. Everything smelled of sheep on Paradise Creek, but there were no sheep in sight. I fished down from the ranger station where there was a huge monument to the Civilian Conservation Corps.

It was a twelve-foot high marble statue of a young man walking out on a cold morning to a crapper that had the classic half-moon cut above the door.

The 1930s will never come again, but his shoes were wet with dew. They'll stay that way in marble.

I went off into the marsh. There the creek was soft and spread out in the grass like a beer belly. The fishing was difficult. Summer ducks were jumping up into flight. They were big mallards with their Rainier Ale-like offspring.

I believe I saw a woodcock. He had a long bill like putting a fire hydrant into a pencil sharpener, then pasting it onto a bird and letting the bird fly away in front of me with this thing on its face for no other purpose than to amaze me.

I worked my way slowly out of the marsh until the creek again became a muscular thing, the strongest Paradise Creek in the world. I was then close enough to see the sheep. There were hundreds of them.

Everything smelled of sheep. The dandelions were suddenly more sheep than flower, each petal reflecting wool and
the sound of a bell ringing off the yellow. But the thing that
smelled the most like sheep, was the very sun itself. When
the sun went behind a cloud, the smell of the sheep decreased,
like standing on some old guy's hearing aid, and when the
sun came back again, the smell of the sheep was loud, like
a clap of thunder inside a cup of coffee.

That afternoon the sheep crossed the creek in front of
my hook. They were so close that their shadows fell across
my bait. I practically caught trout up their assholes.

THE CABINET OF
DOCTOR CALIGARI

Once water bugs were my field. I remember that childhood
spring when I studied the winter-long mud puddles of the
Pacific Northwest. I had a fellowship.

My books were a pair of Sears Roebuck boots, ones with
green rubber pages. Most of my classrooms were close to
the shore. That's where the important things were happening and that's where the good things were happening.

Sometimes as experiments I laid boards out into the mud
puddles, so I could look into the deeper water but it was not
nearly as good as the water in close to the shore.

The water bugs were so small I practically had to lay my
vision like a drowned orange on the mud puddle. There is a
romance about fruit floating outside on the water, about
apples and pears in rivers and lakes. For the first minute
or so, I saw nothing, and then slowly the water bugs came
into being.

I saw a black one with big teeth chasing a white one with
a bag of newspapers slung over its shoulder, two white ones
playing cards near the window, a fourth white one staring
back with a harmonica in its mouth.

I was a scholar until the mud puddles went dry and then I
picked cherries for two-and-a-half cents a pound in an old
orchard that was beside a long, hot dusty road.

The cherry boss was a middle-aged woman who was a real
Okie. Wearing a pair of goofy overalls, her name was Rebel
Smith, and she'd been a friend of "Pretty Boy" Floyd's down
in Oklahoma. "I remember one afternoon 'Pretty Boy' came
driving up in his car. I ran out onto the front porch."

Rebel Smith was always smoking cigarettes and showing
people how to pick cherries and assigning them to trees and
writing down everything in a little book she carried in her
shirt pocket. She smoked just half a cigarette and then threw

51

the other half on the ground.

For the first few days of the picking, I was always seeing
her half-smoked cigarettes lying all over the orchard, near
the john and around the trees and down the rows.

Then she hired half-a-dozen bums to pick cherries because the picking was going too slowly. Rebel picked the
bums up on skidrow every morning and drove them out to
the orchard in a rusty old truck. There were always half-a-
dozen bums, but sometimes they had different faces.

After they came to pick cherries I never saw any more of
her half-smoked cigarettes lying around. They were gone
before they hit the ground. Looking back on it, you might
say that Rebel Smith was anti-mud puddle, but then you might
not say that at all.

THE SALT CREEK COYOTES

High and lonesome and steady, it's the smell of sheep down in the valley that has done it to them. Here all afternoon in the rain I've been listening to the sound of the coyotes up on Salt Creek.

The smell of the sheep grazing in the valley has done it to them. Their voices water and come down the canyon, past the summer homes. Their voices are a creek, running down the mountain, over the bones of sheep, living and dead.

O, THERE ARE COYOTES UP ON SALT CREEK so the sign on the trail says, and it also says, WATCH OUT FOR CYANIDE CAPSULES PUT ALONG THE CREEK TO KILL COYOTES. DON'T PICK THEM UP AND EAT THEM. NOT UNLESS YOU'RE A COYOTE. THEY'LL KILL YOU. LEAVE THEM ALONE.

Then the sign says this all over again in Spanish. ¡ AH! HAY COYOTES EN SALT CREEK, TAMBIEN. CUIDADO CON LAS CAPSULAS DE CIANURO: MATAN. NO LAS COMA; A MENOS QUE SEA VD. UN COYOTE. MATAN. NO LAS TOQUE.

It does not say it in Russian.

I asked an old guy in a bar about those cyanide capsules up on Salt Creek and he told me that they were a kind of pistol. They put a pleasing coyote scent on the trigger (probably the smell of a coyote snatch) and then a coyote comes along and gives it a good sniff, a fast feel and BLAM! That's all, brother.

I went fishing up on Salt Creek and caught a nice little Dolly Varden trout, spotted and slender as a snake you'd expect to find in a jewelry store, but after a while I could think only of the gas chamber at San Quentin.

O Caryl Chessman and Alexander Robillard Vistas! as if they were names for tracts of three-bedroom houses with wall-to-wall carpets and plumbing that defies the imagination.

Then it came to me up there on Salt Creek, capital punishment being what it is, an act of state business with no song down the railroad track after the train has gone and no vibration on the rails, that they should take the head of a coyote killed by one of those God-damn cyanide things up on Salt Creek and hollow it out and dry it in the sun and then make it into a crown with the teeth running in a circle around the top of it and a nice green light coming off the teeth.

Then the witnesses and newspapermen and gas chamber flunkies would have to watch a king wearing a coyote crown die there in front of them, the gas rising in the chamber like a rain mist drifting down the mountain from Salt Creek. It has been raining here now for two days, and through the trees, the heart stops beating.

THE HUNCHBACK TROUT

The creek was made narrow by little green trees that grew too close together. The creek was like 12,845 telephone booths in a row with high Victorian ceilings and all the doors taken off and all the backs of the booths knocked out.

Sometimes when I went fishing in there, I felt just like a telephone repairman, even though I did not look like one. I was only a kid covered with fishing tackle, but in some strange way by going in there and catching a few trout, I kept the telephones in service. I was an asset to society.

It was pleasant work, but at times it made me uneasy. It could grow dark in there instantly when there were some clouds in the sky and they worked their way onto the sun. Then you almost needed candles to fish by, and foxfire in your reflexes.

Once I was in there when it started raining. It was dark and hot and steamy. I was of course on overtime. I had that going in my favor. I caught seven trout in fifteen minutes.

The trout in those telephone booths were good fellows. There were a lot of young cutthroat trout six to nine inches long, perfect pan size for local calls. Sometimes there were a few fellows, eleven inches or so—for the long distance calls.

I've always liked cutthroat trout. They put up a good fight, running against the bottom and then broad jumping. Under their throats they fly the orange banner of Jack the Ripper.

Also in the creek were a few stubborn rainbow trout, seldom heard from, but there all the same, like certified public accountants. I'd catch one every once in a while. They were fat and chunky, almost as wide as they were long. I've heard those trout called "squire" trout.

It used to take me about an hour to hitchhike to that creek. There was a river nearby. The river wasn't much. The creek

55

was where I punched in. Leaving my card above the clock, I'd punch out again when it was time to go home.

I remember the afternoon I caught the hunchback trout.

A farmer gave me a ride in a truck. He picked me up at a traffic signal beside a bean field and he never said a word to me.

His stopping and picking me up and driving me down the road was as automatic a thing to him as closing the barn door, nothing need be said about it, but still I was in motion traveling thirty-five miles an hour down the road, watching houses and groves of trees go by, watching chickens and mailboxes enter and pass through my vision.

Then I did not see any houses for a while. "This is where I get out," I said.

The farmer nodded his head. The truck stopped.

"Thanks a lot," I said.

The farmer did not ruin his audition for the Metropolitan Opera by making a sound. He just nodded his head again. The truck started up. He was the original silent old farmer.

A little while later I was punching in at the creek. I put my card above the clock and went into that long tunnel of telephone booths.

I waded about seventy-three telephone booths in. I caught two trout in a little hole that was like a wagon wheel. It was one of my favorite holes, and always good for a trout or two.

I always like to think of that hole as a kind of pencil sharpener. I put my reflexes in and they came back out with a good point on them. Over a period of a couple of years, I must have caught fifty trout in that hole, though it was only as big as a wagon wheel.

I was fishing with salmon eggs and using a size 14 single egg hook on a pound and a quarter test tippet. The two trout lay in my creel covered entirely by green ferns, ferns made gentle and fragile by the damp walls of telephone booths.

The next good place was forty-five telephone booths in. The place was at the end of a run of gravel, brown and slippery with algae. The run of gravel dropped off and disappeared at a little shelf where there were some white rocks.

One of the rocks was kind of strange. It was a flat white rock. Off by itself from the other rocks, it reminded me of a white cat I had seen in my childhood.

The cat had fallen or been thrown off a high wooden side-

56

walk that went along the side of a hill in Tacoma, Washington. The cat was lying in a parking lot below.

The fall had not appreciably helped the thickness of the cat, and then a few people had parked their cars on the cat. Of course, that was a long time ago and the cars looked different from the way they look now.

You hardly see those cars any more. They are the old cars. They have to get off the highway because they can't keep up.

That flat white rock off by itself from the other rocks reminded me of that dead cat come to lie there in the creek, among 12,845 telephone booths.

I threw out a salmon egg and let it drift down over that rock and WHAM! a good hit! and I had the fish on and it ran hard downstream, cutting at an angle and staying deep and really coming on hard, solid and uncompromising, and then the fish jumped and for a second I thought it was a frog. I'd never seen a fish like that before.

God-damn! What the hell!

The fish ran deep again and I could feel its life energy screaming back up the line to my hand. The line felt like sound. It was like an ambulance siren coming straight at me, red light flashing, and then going away again and then taking to the air and becoming an air-raid siren.

The fish jumped a few more times and it still looked like a frog, but it didn't have any legs. Then the fish grew tired and sloppy, and I swung and splashed it up the surface of the creek and into my net.

The fish was a twelve-inch rainbow trout with a huge hump on its back. A hunchback trout. The first I'd ever seen. The hump was probably due to an injury that occurred when the trout was young. Maybe a horse stepped on it or a tree fell over in a storm or its mother spawned where they were building a bridge.

There was a fine thing about that trout. I only wish I could have made a death mask of him. Not of his body though, but of his energy. I don't know if anyone would have understood his body. I put it in my creel.

Later in the afternoon when the telephone booths began to grow dark at the edges, I punched out of the creek and went home. I had that hunchback trout for dinner. Wrapped in cornmeal and fried in butter, its hump tasted sweet as the kisses of Esmeralda.

THE TEDDY ROOSEVELT
CHINGADER'

The Challis National Forest was created July 1, 1908, by
Executive Order of President Theodore Roosevelt . . .
Twenty Million years ago, scientists tell us, three-toed
horses, camels, and possibly rhinoceroses were plentiful
in this section of the country.

This is part of my history in the Challis National Forest.
We came over through Lowman after spending a little time
with my woman's Mormon relatives at McCall, where we
learned about Spirit Prison and couldn't find Duck Lake.

I carried the baby up the mountain. The sign said $1^1/2$
miles. There was a green sports car parked on the road.
We walked up the trail until we met a man with a green
sports car hat on and a girl in a light summer dress.

She had her dress rolled above her knees and when she
saw us coming, she rolled her dress down. The man had a
bottle of wine in his back pocket. The wine was in a long
green bottle. It looked funny sticking out of his back pocket.

"How far is it to Spirit Prison?" I asked.

"You're about half way," he said.

The girl smiled. She had blonde hair and they went on
down. Bounce, bounce, bounce, like a pair of birthday balls,
down through the trees and boulders.

I put the baby down in a patch of snow lying in the hollow
behind a big stump. She played in the snow and then started
eating it. I remembered something from a book by Justice
of the Supreme Court, William O. Douglas. DON'T EAT
SNOW. IT'S BAD FOR YOU AND WILL GIVE YOU A STOM-
ACH ACHE.

"Stop eating that snow!" I said to the baby.

I put her on my shoulders and continued up the path toward
Spirit Prison. That's where everybody who isn't a Mormon

goes when they die. All Catholics, Buddhists, Moslems, Jews, Baptists, Methodists and International Jewel Thieves. Everybody who isn't a Mormon goes to the Spirit Slammer.

The sign said $1^1/2$ miles. The path was easy to follow, then it just stopped. We lost it near a creek. I looked all around. I looked on both sides of the creek, but the path had just vanished.

Could be the fact that we were still alive had something to do with it. Hard to tell.

We turned around and started back down the mountain. The baby cried when she saw the snow again, holding out her hands for the snow. We didn't have time to stop. It was getting late.

We got in our car and drove back to McCall. That evening we talked about Communism. The Mormon girl read aloud to us from a book called The Naked Communist written by an ex-police chief of Salt Lake City.

My woman asked the girl if she believed the book were written under the influence of Divine Power, if she considered the book to be a religious text of some sort.

The girl said, "No."

I bought a pair of tennis shoes and three pairs of socks at a store in McCall. The socks had a written guarantee. I tried to save the guarantee, but I put it in my pocket and lost it. The guarantee said that if anything happened to the socks within three months time, 1 would get new socks. It seemed like a good idea.

I was supposed to launder the old socks and send them in with the guarantee. Right off the bat, new socks would be on their way, traveling across America with my name on the package. Then all I would have to do, would be to open the package, take those new socks out and put them on. They would look good on my feet.

I wish I hadn't lost that guarantee. That was a shame. I've had to face the fact that new socks are not going to be a family heirloom. Losing the guarantee took care of that. All future generations are on their own.

We left McCall the next day, the day after I lost the sock guarantee, following the muddy water of the North Fork of the Payette down and the clear water of the South Fork up.

We stopped at Lowman and had a strawberry milkshake and then drove back into the mountains along Clear Creek and over the summit to Bear Creek.

59

There were signs nailed to the trees all along Bear
Creek, the signs said, "IF YOU FISH IN THIS CREEK,
WE'LL HIT YOU IN THE HEAD." I didn't want to be hit in
the head, so I kept my fishing tackle right there in the car.

We saw a flock of sheep. There's a sound that the baby
makes when she sees furry animals. She also makes that
sound when she sees her mother and me naked. She made
that sound and we drove out of the sheep like an airplane
flies out of the clouds.

We entered Challis National Forest about five miles
away from that sound. Driving now along Valley Creek, we
saw the Sawtooth Mountains for the first time. It was cloud-
ing over and we thought it was going to rain.

"Looks like it's raining in Stanley," I said, though I had
never been in Stanley before. It is easy to say things about
Stanley when you have never been there. We saw the road to
Bull Trout Lake. The road looked good. When we reached
Stanley, the streets were white and dry like a collision at a
high rate of speed between a cemetery and a truck loaded
with sacks of flour.

We stopped at a store in Stanley. I bought a candy bar and
asked how the trout fishing was in Cuba. The woman at the
store said, "You're better off dead, you Commie bastard."
I got a receipt for the candy bar to be used for income tax
purposes.

The old ten-cent deduction.

I didn't learn anything about fishing in that store. The
people were awfully nervous, especially a young man who
was folding overalls. He had about a hundred pairs left to
fold and he was really nervous.

We went over to a restaurant and I had a hamburger and
my woman had a cheeseburger and the baby ran in circles
like a bat at the World's Fair.

There was a girl there in her early teens or maybe she
was only ten years old. She wore lipstick and had a loud
voice and seemed to be aware of boys. She got a lot of fun
out of sweeping the front porch of the restaurant.

She came in and played around with the baby. She was
very good with the baby. Her voice dropped down and got
soft with the baby. She told us that her father'd had a heart
attack and was still in bed. "He can't get up and around,"
she said.

60

We had some more coffee and I thought about the Mormons. That very morning we had said good-bye to them, after having drunk coffee in their house.

The smell of coffee had been like a spider web in the house. It had not been an easy smell. It had not lent itself to religious contemplation, thoughts of temple work to be done in Salt Lake, dead relatives to be discovered among ancient papers in Illinois and Germany. Then more temple work to be done in Salt Lake.

The Mormon woman told us that when she had been married in the temple at Salt Lake, a mosquito had bitten her on the wrist just before the ceremony and her wrist had swollen up and become huge and just awful. It could've been seen through the lace by a blindman. She had been so embarrassed.

She told us that those Salt Lake mosquitoes always made her swell up when they bit her. Last year, she had told us, she'd been in Salt Lake, doing some temple work for a dead relative when a mosquito had bitten her and her whole body had swollen up. "I felt so embarrassed," she had told us. "Walking around like a balloon."

We finished our coffee and left. Not a drop of rain had fallen in Stanley. It was about an hour before sundown.

We drove up to Big Redfish Lake, about four miles from Stanley and looked it over. Big Redfish Lake is the Forest Lawn of camping in Idaho, laid out for maximum comfort. There were a lot of people camped there, and some of them looked as if they had been camped there for a long time.

We decided that we were too young to camp at Big Redfish Lake, and besides they charged fifty cents a day, three dollars a week like a skidrow hotel, and there were just too many people there. There were too many trailers and campers parked in the halls. We couldn't get to the elevator because there was a family from New York parked there in a ten-room trailer.

Three children came by drinking rub-a-dub and pulling an old granny by her legs. Her legs were straight out and stiff and her butt was banging on the carpet. Those kids were pretty drunk and the old granny wasn't too sober either, shouting something like, "Let the Civil War come again, I'm ready to fuck!"

We went down to Little Redfish Lake. The campgrounds there were just about abandoned. There were so many people

61

up at Big Redfish Lake and practically nobody camping at Little Redfish Lake, and it was free, too.

We wondered what was wrong with the camp. If perhaps a camping plague, a sure destroyer that leaves all your camping equipment, your car and your sex organs in tatters like old sails, had swept the camp just a few days before, and those few people who were staying at the camp now, were staying there because they didn't have any sense.

We joined them enthusiastically. The camp had a beautiful view of the mountains. We found a place that really looked good, right on the lake.

Unit 4 had a stove. It was a square metal box mounted on a cement block. There was a stove pipe on top of the box, but there were no bullet holes in the pipe. I was amazed. Almost all the camp stoves we had seen in Idaho had been full of bullet holes. I guess it's only reasonable that people, when they get the chance, would want to shoot some old stove sitting in the woods.

Unit 4 had a big wooden table with benches attached to it like a pair of those old Benjamin Franklin glasses, the ones with those funny square lenses. I sat down on the left lens, facing the Sawtooth Mountains. Like astigmatism, I made myself at home.

FOOTNOTE CHAPTER TO "THE SHIPPING OF TROUT FISHING IN AMERICA SHORTY TO NELSON ALGREN"

Well, well, Trout Fishing in America Shorty's back in town, but I don't think it's going to be the same as it was before. Those good old days are over because Trout Fishing in America Shorty is famous. The movies have discovered him.

Last week "The New Wave" took him out of his wheelchair and laid him out in a cobblestone alley. Then they shot some footage of him. He ranted and raved and they put it down on film.

Later on, probably, a different voice will be dubbed in. It will be a noble and eloquent voice denouncing man's inhumanity to man in no uncertain terms.

"Trout Fishing in America Shorty, Mon Amour."

His soliloquy beginning with, "I was once a famous skiptracer known throughout America as 'Grasshopper Nijinsky.' Nothing was too good for me. Beautiful blondes followed me wherever I went." Etc. . . . They'll milk it for all it's worth and make cream and butter from a pair of empty pants legs and a low budget.

But I may be all wrong. What was being shot may have been just a scene from a new science-fiction movie "Trout Fishing in America Shorty from Outer Space." One of those cheap thrillers with the theme: Scientists, mad-or-otherwise, should never play God, that ends with the castle on fire and a lot of people walking home through the dark woods.

THE PUDDING MASTER OF
STANLEY BASIN

Tree, snow and rock beginnings, the mountain in back of the lake promised us eternity, but the lake itself was filled with thousands of silly minnows, swimming close to the shore and busy putting in hours of Mack Sennett time.

The minnows were an Idaho tourist attraction. They should have been made into a National Monument. Swimming close to shore, like children, they believed in their own immortality.

A third-year student in engineering at the University of Montana attempted to catch some of the minnows but he went about it all wrong. So did the children who came on the Fourth of July weekend.

The children waded out into the lake and tried to catch the minnows with their hands. They also used milk cartons and plastic bags. They presented the lake with hours of human effort. Their total catch was one minnow. It jumped out of a can full of water on their table and died under the table, gasping for watery breath while their mother fried eggs on the Coleman stove.

The mother apologized. She was supposed to be watching the fish —THIS IS MY EARTHLY FAILURE— holding the dead fish by the tail, the fish taking all the bows like a young Jewish comedian talking about Adlai Stevenson.

The third-year student in engineering at the University of Montana took a tin can and punched an elaborate design of holes in the can, the design running around and around in circles, like a dog with a fire hydrant in its mouth. Then he attached some string to the can and put a huge salmon egg and a piece of Swiss cheese in the can. After two hours of intimate and universal failure, he went back to Missoula, Montana.

The woman who travels with me discovered the best way to catch the minnows. She used a large pan that had in its bottom the dregs of a distant vanilla pudding. She put the pan in the shallow water along the shore and instantly, hundreds of minnows gathered around. Then, mesmerized by the vanilla pudding, they swam like a children's crusade into the pan. She caught twenty fish with one dip. She put the pan full of fish on the shore and the baby played with the fish for an hour.

We watched the baby to make sure she was just leaning on them a little. We didn't want her to kill any of them because she was too young.

Instead of making her furry sound, she adapted rapidly to the difference between animals and fish, and was soon making a silver sound.

She caught one of the fish with her hand and looked at it for a while. We took the fish out of her hand and put it back into the pan. After a while she was putting the fish back by herself.

Then she grew tired of this. She tipped the pan over and a dozen fish flopped out onto the shore. The children's game and the banker's game, she picked up those silver things, one at a time, and put them back in the pan. There was still a little water in it. The fish liked this. You could tell.

When she got tired of the fish, we put them back in the lake, and they were all quite alive, but nervous. I doubt if they will ever want vanilla pudding again.

ROOM 208, HOTEL

TROUT FISHING IN AMERICA

Half a block from Broadway and Columbus is Hotel Trout Fishing in America, a cheap hotel. It is very old and run by some Chinese. They are young and ambitious Chinese and the lobby is filled with the smell of Lysol.

The Lysol sits like another guest on the stuffed furniture, reading a copy of the Chronicle, the Sports Section. It is the only furniture I have ever seen in my life that looks like baby food.

And the Lysol sits asleep next to an old Italian pensioner who listens to the heavy ticking of the clock and dreams of eternity's golden pasta, sweet basil and Jesus Christ.

The Chinese are always doing something to the hotel. One week they paint a lower banister and the next week they put some new wallpaper on part of the third floor.

No matter how many times you pass that part of the third floor, you cannot remember the color of the wallpaper or what the design is. All you know is that part of the wallpaper is new. It is different from the old wallpaper. But you cannot remember what that looks like either.

One day the Chinese take a bed out of a room and lean it up against the wall. It stays there for a month. You get used to seeing it and then you go by one day and it is gone. You wonder where it went.

I remember the first time I went inside Hotel Trout Fishing in America. It was with a friend to meet some people.

"I'll tell you what's happening," he said. "She's an ex-hustler who works for the telephone company. He went to medical school for a while during the Great Depression and then he went into show business. After that, he was an errand boy for an abortion mill in Los Angeles. He took a fall and did some time in San Quentin.

66

"I think you'll like them. They're good people.

"He met her a couple of years ago in North Beach. She was hustling for a spade pimp. It's kind of weird. Most women have the temperament to be a whore, but she's one of these rare women who just don't have it—the whore temperament. She's Negro, too.

"She was a teenage girl living on a farm in Oklahoma. The pimp drove by one afternoon and saw her playing in the front yard. He stopped his car and got out and talked to her father for a while.

"I guess he gave her father some money. He came up with something good because her father told her to go and get her things. So she went with the pimp. Simple as that.

"He took her to San Francisco and turned her out and she hated it. He kept her in line by terrorizing her all the time. He was a real sweetheart.

"She had some brains, so he got her a job with the telephone company during the day, and he had her hustling at night.

"When Art took her away from him, he got pretty mad. A good thing and all that. He used to break into Art's hotel room in the middle of the night and put a switchblade to Art's throat and rant and rave. Art kept putting bigger and bigger locks on the door, but the pimp just kept breaking in—a huge fellow.

"So Art went out and got a .32 pistol, and the next time the pimp broke in, Art pulled the gun out from underneath the covers and jammed it into the pimp's mouth and said, 'You'll be out of luck the next time you come through that door, Jack.' This broke the pimp up. He never went back. The pimp certainly lost a good thing.

"He ran up a couple thousand dollars worth of bills in her name, charge accounts and the like. They're still paying them off.

"The pistol's right there beside the bed, just in case the pimp has an attack of amnesia and wants to have his shoes shined in a funeral parlor.

"When we go up there, he'll drink the wine. She won't. She'll have a little bottle of brandy. She won't offer us any of it. She drinks about four of them a day. Never buys a fifth. She always keeps going out and getting another half-pint.

"That's the way she handles it. She doesn't talk very much,

and she doesn't make any bad scenes. A good-looking woman."

My friend knocked on the door and we could hear somebody get up off the bed and come to the door.

"Who's there?" said a man on the other side.

"Me," my friend said, in a voice deep and recognizable
as any name.

"I'll open the door." A simple declarative sentence. He
undid about a hundred locks, bolts and chains and anchors
and steel spikes and canes filled with acid, and then the
door opened like the classroom of a great university and
everything was in its proper place: the gun beside the bed
and a small bottle of brandy beside an attractive Negro woman.

There were many flowers and plants growing in the room,
some of them were on the dresser, surrounded by old photographs. All of the photographs were of white people, including Art when he was young and handsome and looked just like
the 1930s.

There were pictures of animals cut out of magazines and
tacked to the wall, with crayola frames drawn around them
and crayola picture wires drawn holding them to the wall.
They were pictures of kittens and puppies. They looked just
fine.

There was a bowl of goldfish next to the bed, next to the
gun. How religious and intimate the goldfish and the gun
looked together.

They had a cat named 208. They covered the bathroom
floor with newspaper and the cat crapped on the newspaper.
My friend said that 208 thought he was the only cat left in the
world, not having seen another cat since he was a tiny kitten.
They never let him out of the room. He was a red cat and
very aggressive. When you played with that cat, he really
bit you. Stroke 208's fur and he'd try to disembowel your
hand as if it were a belly stuffed full of extrasoft intestines.

We sat there and drank and talked about books. Art had
owned a lot of books in Los Angeles, but they were all gone
now. He told us that he used to spend his spare time in sec-
ondhand bookstores buying old and unusual books when he
was in show business, traveling from city to city across
America. Some of them were very rare autographed books,
he told us, but he had bought them for very little and was
forced to sell them for very little.

"They'd be worth a lot of money now," he said.

The Negro woman sat there very quietly studying her brandy. A couple of times she said yes, in a sort of nice way. She used the word yes to its best advantage, when surrounded by no meaning and left alone from other words.

They did their own cooking in the room and had a single hot plate sitting on the floor, next to half a dozen plants, including a peach tree growing in a coffee can. Their closet was stuffed with food. Along with shirts, suits and dresses, were canned goods, eggs and cooking oil.

My friend told me that she was a very fine cook. That she could really cook up a good meal, fancy dishes, too, on that single hot plate, next to the peach tree.

They had a good world going for them. He had such a soft voice and manner that he worked as a private nurse for rich mental patients. He made good money when he worked, but sometimes he was sick himself. He was kind of run down. She was still working for the telephone company, but she wasn't doing that night work any more.

They were still paying off the bills that pimp had run up. I mean, years had passed and they were still paying them off: a Cadillac and a hi-fi set and expensive clothes and all those things that Negro pimps do love to have.

I went back there half a dozen times after that first meeting. An interesting thing happened. I pretended that the cat, 208, was named after their room number, though I knew that their number was in the three hundreds. The room was on the third floor. It was that simple.

I always went to their room following the geography of Hotel Trout Fishing in America, rather than its numerical layout. I never knew what the exact number of their room was. I knew secretly it was in the three hundreds and that was all.

Anyway, it was easier for me to establish order in my mind by pretending that the cat was named after their room number. It seemed like a good idea and the logical reason for a cat to have the name 208. It, of course, was not true. It was a fib. The cat's name was 208 and the room number was in the three hundreds.

Where did the name 208 come from? What did it mean? I thought about it for a while, hiding it from the rest of my mind. But I didn't ruin my birthday by secretly thinking about it too hard.

A year later I found out the true significance of 208's name, purely by accident. My telephone rang one Saturday morning when the sun was shining on the hills. It was a close friend of mine and he said, "I'm in the slammer. Come and get me out. They're burning black candles around the drunk tank."

I went down to the Hall of Justice to bail my friend out, and discovered that 208 is the room number of the bail office. It was very simple. I paid ten dollars for my friend's life and found the original meaning of 208, how it runs like melting snow all the way down the mountainside to a small cat living and playing in Hotel Trout Fishing in America, believing itself to be the last cat in the world, not having seen another cat in such a long time, totally unafraid, newspaper spread out all over the bathroom floor, and something good cooking on the hot plate.

THE SURGEON

I watched my day begin on Little Redfish Lake as clearly as
the first light of dawn or the first ray of the sunrise, though
the dawn and the sunrise had long since passed and it was
now late in the morning.

The surgeon took a knife from the sheath at his belt and
cut the throat of the chub with a very gentle motion, showing
poetically how sharp the knife was, and then he heaved the
fish back out into the lake.

The chub made an awkward dead splash and obeyed all the
traffic laws of this world SCHOOL ZONE SPEED 25 MILES
and sank to the cold bottom of the lake. It lay there white
belly up like a school bus covered with snow. A trout swam
over and took a look, just putting in time, and swam away.

The surgeon and I were talking about the AMA. I don't
know how in the hell we got on the thing, but we were on it.
Then he wiped the knife off and put it back in the sheath. I
actually don't know how we got on the AMA.

The surgeon said that he had spent twenty-five years becoming a doctor. His studies had been interrupted by the
Depression and two wars. He told me that he would give up
the practice of medicine if it became socialized in America.

"I've never turned away a patient in my life, and I've
never known another doctor who has. Last year I wrote off
six thousand dollars worth of bad debts," he said.

I was going to say that a sick person should never under
any conditions be a bad debt, but I decided to forget it. Nothing was going to be proved or changed on the shores of Little
Redfish Lake, and as that chub had discovered, it was not a
good place to have cosmetic surgery done.

"I worked three years ago for a union in Southern Utah
that had a health plan," the surgeon said. "I would not care

71

to practice medicine under such conditions. The patients
think they own you and your time. They think you're their
own personal garbage can.

"I'd be home eating dinner and the telephone would ring,
'Help! Doctor! I'm dying! It's my stomach! I've got horrible
pains!' I would get up from my dinner and rush over there.

"The guy would meet me at the door with a can of beer in
his hand. 'Hi, doc, come on in. I'll get you a beer. I'm
watching TV. The pain's all gone. Great, huh? I feel like a
million. Sit down. I'll get you a beer, doc. The Ed Sullivan
Show's on.'

"No thank you," the surgeon said. "I wouldn't care to
practice medicine under such conditions. No thank you. No
thanks.

"I like to hunt and I like to fish," he said. "That's why I
moved to Twin Falls. I'd heard so much about Idaho hunting
and fishing. I've been very disappointed. I've given up my
practice, sold my home in Twin, and now I'm looking for a
new place to settle down.

"I've written to Montana, Wyoming, Colorado, New Mexico, Arizona, California, Nevada, Oregon and Washington for
their hunting and fishing regulations, and I'm studying them
all," he said.

"I've got enough money to travel around for six months,
looking for a place to settle down where the hunting and fishing is good. I'll get twelve hundred dollars back in income
tax returns by not working any more this year. That's two
hundred a month for not working. I don't understand this
country," he said.

The surgeon's wife and children were in a trailer nearby.
The trailer had come in the night before, pulled by a brand-
new Rambler station wagon. He had two children, a boy two-
and-a-half years old and the other, an infant born prematurely, but now almost up to normal weight.

The surgeon told me that they'd come over from camping
on Big Lost River where he had caught a fourteen-inch brook
trout. He was young looking, though he did not have much
hair on his head.

I talked to the surgeon for a little while longer and said
good-bye. We were leaving in the afternoon for Lake Josephus,
located at the edge of the Idaho Wilderness, and he was leaving for America, often only a place in the mind.

A NOTE ON THE CAMPING
CRAZE THAT IS CURRENTLY
SWEEPING AMERICA

As much as anything else, the Coleman lantern is the symbol of the camping craze that is currently sweeping America, with its unholy white light burning in the forests of America.

Last summer, a Mr. Norris was drinking at a bar in San Francisco. It was Sunday night and he'd had six or seven. Turning to the guy on the next stool, he said, "What are you up to?"

"Just having a few," the guy said.

"That's what I'm doing," Mr. Norris said. "I like it."

"I know what you mean," the guy said. "I had to lay off for a couple years. I'm just starting up again."

"What was wrong?" Mr. Norris said.

"I had a hole in my liver," the guy said.

"In your liver?"

"Yeah, the doctor said it was big enough to wave a flag in. It's better now. I can have a couple once in a while. I'm not supposed to, but it won't kill me."

"Well, I'm thirty-two years old," Mr. Norris said. "I've had three wives and I can't remember the names of my children."

The guy on the next stool, like a bird on the next island, took a sip from his Scotch and soda. The guy liked the sound of the alcohol in his drink. He put the glass back on the bar.

"That's no problem," he said to Mr. Norris. "The best thing I know for remembering the names of children from previous marriages, is to go out camping, try a little trout fishing. Trout fishing is one of the best things in the world for remembering children's names."

"Is that right?" Mr. Norris said.

"Yeah," the guy said.

"That sounds like an idea," Mr. Norris said. "I've got to do something. Sometimes I think one of them is named Carl, but that's impossible. My third-ex hated the name Carl."

"You try some camping and that trout fishing," the guy
on the next stool said. "And you'll remember the names of
your unborn children."

"Carl! Carl! Your mother wants you!" Mr. Norris yelled
as a kind of joke, then he realized that it wasn't very funny.
He was getting there.

He'd have a couple more and then his head would always
fall forward and hit the bar like a gunshot. He'd always miss
his glass, so he wouldn't cut his face. His head would always
jump up and look startled around the bar, people staring at
it. He'd get up then, and take it home.

The next morning Mr. Norris went down to a sporting
goods store and charged his equipment. He charged a 9 x 9
foot dry finish tent with an aluminum center pole. Then he
charged an Arctic sleeping bag filled with eiderdown and an
air mattress and an air pillow to go with the sleeping bag.
He also charged an air alarm clock to go along with the idea
of night and waking in the morning.

He charged a two-burner Coleman stove and a Coleman
lantern and a folding aluminum table and a big set of inter-
locking aluminum cookware and a portable ice box.

The last things he charged were his fishing tackle and a
bottle of insect repellent.

He left the next day for the mountains.

Hours later, when he arrived in the mountains, the first
sixteen campgrounds he stopped at were filled with people.
He was a little surprised. He had no idea the mountains
would be so crowded.

At the seventeenth campground, a man had just died of a
heart attack and the ambulance attendants were taking down
his tent. They lowered the center pole and then pulled up the
corner stakes. They folded the tent neatly and put it in the
back of the ambulance, right beside the man's body.

They drove off down the road, leaving behind them in the
air, a cloud of brilliant white dust. The dust looked like the
light from a Coleman lantern.

Mr. Norris pitched his tent right there and set up all his
equipment and soon had it all going at once. After he finished
eating a dehydrated beef Stroganoff dinner, he turned off all
his equipment with the master air switch and went to sleep,
for it was now dark.

74

It was about midnight when they brought the body and placed it beside the tent, less than a foot away from where Mr. Norris was sleeping in his Arctic sleeping bag.

He was awakened when they brought the body. They weren't exactly the quietest body bringers in the world. Mr. Norris could see the bulge of the body against the side of the tent. The only thing that separated him from the dead body was a thin layer of 6 oz. water resistant and mildew resistant DRY FINISH green AMERIFLEX poplin.

Mr. Norris un-zipped his sleeping bag and went outside with a gigantic hound-like flashlight. He saw the body bringers walking down the path toward the creek.

"Hey, you guys!" Mr. Norris shouted. "Come back here. You forgot something."

"What do you mean?" one of them said. They both looked very sheepish, caught in the teeth of the flashlight.

"You know what I mean," Mr. Norris said. "Right now!"

The body bringers shrugged their shoulders, looked at each other and then reluctantly went back, dragging their feet like children all the way. They picked up the body. It was heavy and one of them had trouble getting hold of the feet.

That one said, kind of hopelessly to Mr. Norris, "You won't change your mind?"

"Goodnight and good-bye," Mr. Norris said.

They went off down the path toward the creek, carrying the body between them. Mr. Norris turned his flashlight off and he could hear them, stumbling over the rocks along the bank of the creek. He could hear them swearing at each other. He heard one of them say, "Hold your end up." Then he couldn't hear anything.

About ten minutes later he saw all sorts of lights go on at another campsite down along the creek. He heard a distant voice shouting, "The answer is no! You already woke up the kids. They have to have their rest. We're going on a four-mile hike tomorrow up to Fish Konk Lake. Try someplace else."

A RETURN TO THE COVER OF
THIS BOOK

Dear Trout Fishing in America:

I met your friend Fritz in Washington Square. He told me to tell you that his case went to a jury and that he was acquitted by the jury.

He said that it was important for me to say that his case went to a jury and that he was acquitted by the jury, so I've said it again.

He looked in good shape. He was sitting in the sun. There's an old San Francisco saying that goes: "It's better to rest in Washington Square than in the California Adult Authority."

How are things in New York?

Yours,

"An Ardent Admirer"

Dear Ardent Admirer:

It's good to hear that Fritz isn't in jail. He was very worried about it. The last time I was in San Francisco, he told me he thought the odds were 10-1 in favor of him going away. I told him to get a good lawyer. It appears that he followed my advice and also was very lucky. That's always a good combination.

You asked about New York and New York is very hot.

I'm visiting some friends, a young burglar and his wife. He's unemployed and his wife is working as a cocktail waitress. He's been looking for work but I fear the worst.

It was so hot last night that I slept with a wet sheet wrapped around myself, trying to keep cool. I felt like a mental patient.

I woke up in the middle of the night and the room was filled with steam rising off the sheet, and there was jungle stuff,

76

abandoned equipment and tropical flowers, on the floor and on the furniture.

I took the sheet into the bathroom and plopped it into the tub and turned the cold water on it. Their dog came in and started barking at me.

The dog barked so loud that the bathroom was soon filled with dead people. One of them wanted to use my wet sheet for a shroud. I said no, and we got into a big argument over it and woke up the Puerto Ricans in the next apartment, and they began pounding on the walls.

The dead people all left in a huff. "We know when we're not wanted," one of them said.

"You're damn tootin'," I said.

I've had enough.

I'm going to get out of New York. Tomorrow I'm leaving for Alaska. I'm going to find an ice-cold creek near the Arctic where that strange beautiful moss grows and spend a week with the grayling. My address will be, Trout Fishing in America, c/o General Delivery, Fairbanks, Alaska.

Your friend,

Trout Fishing in America

THE LAKE JOSEPHUS DAYS

We left Little Redfish for Lake Josephus, traveling along the good names—from Stanley to Capehorn to Seafoam to the Rapid River, up Float Creek, past the Greyhound Mine and then to Lake Josephus, and a few days after that up the trail to Hell-diver Lake with the baby on my shoulders and a good limit of trout waiting in Hell-diver.

Knowing the trout would wait there like airplane tickets for us to come, we stopped at Mushroom Springs and had a drink of cold shadowy water and some photographs taken of the baby and me sitting together on a log.

I hope someday we'll have enough money to get those pictures developed. Sometimes I get curious about them, wondering if they will turn out all right. They are in suspension now like seeds in a package. I'll be older when they are developed and easier to please. Look there's the baby! Look there's Mushroom Springs! Look there's me!

I caught the limit of trout within an hour of reaching Hell-diver, and my woman, in all the excitement of good fishing, let the baby fall asleep directly in the sun and when the baby woke up, she puked and I carried her back down the trail.

My woman trailed silently behind, carrying the rods and the fish. The baby puked a couple more times, thimblefuls of gentle lavender vomit, but still it got on my clothes, and her face was hot and flushed.

We stopped at Mushroom Springs. I gave her a small drink of water, not too much, and rinsed the vomit taste out of her mouth. Then I wiped the puke off my clothes and for some strange reason suddenly it was a perfect time, there at Mushroom Springs, to wonder whatever happened to the Zoot suit.

Along with World War II and the Andrews Sisters, the Zoot suit had been very popular in the early 40s. I guess

78

they were all just passing fads.

A sick baby on the trail down from Hell-diver, July 1961, is probably a more important question. It cannot be left to go on forever, a sick baby to take her place in the galaxy, among the comets, bound to pass close to the earth every 173 years.

She stopped puking after Mushroom Springs, and I carried her back down along the path in and out of the shadows and across other nameless springs, and by the time we got down to Lake Josephus, she was all right.

She was soon running around with a big cutthroat trout in her hands, carrying it like a harp on her way to a concert— ten minutes late with no bus in sight and no taxi either.

TROUT FISHING

ON THE STREET OF ETERNITY

<u>Calle de Eternidad</u>: We walked up from Gelatao, birthplace
of Benito Juarez. Instead of taking the road we followed a
path up along the creek. Some boys from the school in Gela-
tao told us that up along the creek was the shortcut.

The creek was clear but a little milky, and as I remember the path was steep in places. We met people coming down
the path because it was really the shortcut. They were all
Indians carrying something.

Finally the path went away from the creek and we climbed
a hill and arrived at the cemetery. It was a very old cemetery and kind of run down with weeds and death growing there
like partners in a dance.

There was a cobblestone street leading up from the cemetery to the town of Ixtlan, pronounced East-LON, on top of
another hill. There were no houses along the street until you
reached the town.

In the hair of the world, the street was very steep as you
went up into Ixtlan. There was a street sign that pointed back
down toward the cemetery, following every cobblestone with
loving care all the way.

We were still out of breath from the climb. The sign said
Calle de Eternidad. Pointing.

I was not always a world traveler, visiting exotic places
in Southern Mexico. Once I was just a kid working for an old
woman in the Pacific Northwest. She was in her nineties and
I worked for her on Saturdays and after school and during the
summer.

Sometimes she would make me lunch, little egg sandwiches with the crusts cut off as if by a surgeon, and she'd give
me slices of banana dunked in mayonnaise.

The old woman lived by herself in a house that was like a

twin sister to her. The house was four stories high and had
at least thirty rooms and the old lady was five feet high and
weighed about eighty-two pounds.

She had a big radio from the 1920s in the living room and
it was the only thing in the house that looked remotely as if
it had come from this century, and then there was still a
doubt in my mind.

A lot of cars, airplanes and vacuum cleaners and refrig-
erators and things that come from the 1920s look as if they
had come from the 1890s. It's the beauty of our speed that
has done it to them, causing them to age prematurely into the
clothes and thoughts of people from another century.

The old woman had an old dog, but he hardly counted any
more. He was so old that he looked like a stuffed dog. Once
I took him for a walk down to the store. It was just like taking a stuffed dog for a walk. I tied him up to a stuffed fire
hydrant and he pissed on it, but it was only stuffed piss.

I went into the store and bought some stuffing for the old
lady. Maybe a pound of coffee or a quart of mayonnaise.

I did things for her like chop the Canadian thistles. During the 1920s (or was it the 1890s) she was motoring in California, and her husband stopped the car at a filling station
and told the attendant to fill it up.

"How about some wild flower seeds?" the attendant said.

"No," her husband said. "Gasoline."

"I know that, sir," the attendant said. "But we're giving
away wild flower seeds with the gasoline today."

"All right," her husband said. "Give us some wild flower
seeds, then. But be sure and fill the car up with gasoline.
Gasoline's what I really want."

"They'll brighten up your garden, sir."

"The gasoline?"

"No, sir, the flowers."

They returned to the Northwest, planted the seeds and
they were Canadian thistles. Every year I chopped them down
and they always grew back. I poured chemicals on them and
they always grew back.

Curses were music to their roots. A blow on the back of
the neck was like a harpsichord to them. Those Canadian
thistles were there for keeps. Thank you, California, for
your beautiful wild flowers. I chopped them down every year.

I did other things for her like mow the lawn with a grim

old lawnmower. When I first went to work for her, she told me to be careful with that lawnmower. Some itinerant had stopped at her place a few weeks before, asked for some work so he could rent a hotel room and get something to eat, and she'd said, "You can mow the lawn."

"Thanks, ma'am," he'd said and went out and promptly cut three fingers off his right hand with that medieval machine.

I was always very careful with that lawnmower, knowing that somewhere on that place, the ghosts of three fingers were living it up in the grand spook manner. They needed no company from my fingers. My fingers looked just great, right there on my hands.

I cleaned out her rock garden and deported snakes whenever I found them on her place. She told me to kill them, but I couldn't see any percentage in wasting a gartersnake. But I had to get rid of the things because she always promised me she'd have a heart attack if she ever stepped on one of them.

So I'd catch them and deport them to a yard across the street, where nine old ladies probably had heart attacks and died from finding those snakes in their toothbrushes. Fortunately, I was never around when their bodies were taken away.

I'd clean the blackberry bushes out of the lilac bushes. Once in a while she'd give me some lilacs to take home, and they were always fine-looking lilacs, and I always felt good, walking down the street, holding the lilacs high and proud like glasses of that famous children's drink: the good flower wine.

I'd chop wood for her stove. She cooked on a woodstove and heated the place during the winter with a huge wood furnace that she manned like the captain of a submarine in a dark basement ocean during the winter.

In the summer I'd throw endless cords of wood into her basement until I was silly in the head and everything looked like wood, even clouds in the sky and cars parked on the street and cats.

There were dozens of little tiny things that I did for her. Find a lost screwdriver, lost in 1911. Pick her a pan full of pie cherries in the spring, and pick the rest of the cherries on the tree for myself. Prune those goofy, at best half-assed trees in the backyard. The ones that grew beside an old pile of lumber. Weed.

One early autumn day she loaned me to the woman next door and I fixed a small leak in the roof of her woodshed. The woman gave me a dollar tip, and I said thank you, and the next time it rained, all the newspapers she had been saving for seventeen years to start fires with got soaking wet. From then on out, I received a sour look every time I passed her house. I was lucky I wasn't lynched.

I didn't work for the old lady in the winter. I'd finish the year by the last of October, raking up leaves or something or transporting the last muttering gartersnake to winter quarters in the old ladies' toothbrush Valhalla across the street.

Then she'd call me on the telephone in the spring. I would always be surprised to hear her little voice, surprised that she was still alive. I'd get on my horse and go out to her place and the whole thing would begin again and I'd make a few bucks and stroke the sun-warmed fur of her stuffed dog.

One spring day she had me ascend to the attic and clean up some boxes of stuff and throw out some stuff and put some stuff back into its imaginary proper place.

I was up there all alone for three hours. It was my first time up there and my last, thank God. The attic was stuffed to the gills with stuff.

Everything that's old in this world was up there. I spent most of my time just looking around.

An old trunk caught my eye. I unstrapped the straps, unclicked the various clickers and opened the God-damn thing. It was stuffed with old fishing tackle. There were old rods and reels and lines and boots and creels and there was a metal box full of flies and lures and hooks.

Some of the hooks still had worms on them. The worms were years and decades old and petrified to the hooks. The worms were now as much a part of the hooks as the metal itself.

There was some old Trout Fishing in America armor in the trunk and beside a weather-beaten fishing helmet, I saw an old diary. I opened the diary to the first page and it said:

The Trout Fishing Diary of Alonso Hagen

It seemed to me that was the name of the old lady's brother who had died of a strange ailment in his youth, a thing I found out by keeping my ears open and looking at a large photograph prominently displayed in her front room.

I turned to the next page in the old diary and it had in columns:

The Trips and The Trout Lost

April	7, 1891	Trout Lost	8
April	15, 1891	Trout Lost	6
April	23, 1891	Trout Lost	12
May	13, 1891	Trout Lost	9
May	23, 1891	Trout Lost	15
May	24, 1891	Trout Lost	10
May	25, 1891	Trout Lost	12
June	2, 1891	Trout Lost	18
June	6, 1891	Trout Lost	15
June	17, 1891	Trout Lost	7
June	19, 1891	Trout Lost	10
June	23, 1891	Trout Lost	14
July	4, 1891	Trout Lost	13
July	23, 1891	Trout Lost	11
August	10, 1891	Trout Lost	13
August	17, 1891	Trout Lost	8
August	20, 1891	Trout Lost	12
August	29, 1891	Trout Lost	21
September	3, 1891	Trout Lost	10
September	11, 1891	Trout Lost	7
September	19, 1891	Trout Lost	5
September	23, 1891	Trout Lost	3

Total Trips 22   Total Trout Lost   239
Average Number of Trout Lost Each Trip 10.8

I turned to the third page and it was just like the preceding page except the year was 1892 and Alonso Hagen went on 24 trips and lost 317 trout for an average of 13.2 trout lost each trip.

The next page was 1893 and the totals were 33 trips and 480 trout lost for an average of 14.5 trout lost each trip.

The next page was 1894. He went on 27 trips, lost 349 trout for an average of 12.9 trout lost each trip.

The next page was 1895. He went on 41 trips, lost 730 trout for an average of 17.8 trout lost each trip.

The next page was 1896. Alonso Hagen only went out 12

times and lost 115 trout for an average of 9.5 trout lost each trip.

The next page was 1897. He went on one trip and lost one trout for an average of one trout lost for one trip.

The last page of the diary was the grand totals for the years running from 1891-1897. Alonso Hagen went fishing 160 times and lost 2,231 trout for a seven-year average of 13.9 trout lost every time he went fishing.

Under the grand totals, there was a little Trout Fishing in America epitaph by Alonso Hagen. It said something like:

"I've had it.

I've gone fishing now for seven years

and I haven't caught a single trout.

I've lost every trout I ever hooked.

They either jump off

or twist off.

or squirm off

or break my leader

or flop off

or fuck off.

I have never even gotten my hands on a trout.

For all its frustration,

I believe it was an interesting experiment

in total loss

but next year somebody else

will have to go trout fishing.

Somebody else will have to go

out there."

THE TOWEL

We came down the road from Lake Josephus and down the
road from Seafoam. We stopped along the way to get a drink
of water. There was a small monument in the forest. I
walked over to the monument to see what was happening. The
glass door of the lookout was partly open and a towel was
hanging on the other side.

At the center of the monument was a photograph. It was
the classic forest lookout photograph I have seen before, from
that America that existed during the 1920s and 30s.

There was a man in the photograph who looked a lot like
Charles A. Lindbergh. He had that same Spirit of St. Louis
nobility and purpose of expression, except that his North Atlantic was the forests of Idaho.

There was a woman cuddled up close to him. She was one
of those great cuddly women of the past, wearing those pants
they used to wear and those hightop, laced boots.

They were standing on the porch of the lookout. The sky was
behind them, no more than a few feet away. People in those days
liked to take that photograph and they liked to be in it.

There were words on the monument. They said:

> "In memory of Charley J. Langer, District
> Forest Ranger, Challis National Forest, Pilot
> Captain Bill Kelly and Co-Pilot Arthur A. Crofts,
> of the U.S. Army killed in an Airplane Crash
> April 5, 1943, near this point while searching
> for survivors of an Army Bomber Crew."

O it's far away now in the mountains that a photograph
guards the memory of a man. The photograph is all alone out
there. The snow is falling eighteen years after his death. It
covers up the door. It covers up the towel.

SANDBOX MINUS JOHN

DILLINGER EQUALS WHAT?

Often I return to the cover of Trout Fishing in America. I
took the baby and went down there this morning. They were
watering the cover with big revolving sprinklers. I saw some
bread lying on the grass. It had been put there to feed the
pigeons.

The old Italians are always doing things like that. The
bread had been turned to paste by the water and was squashed
flat against the grass. Those dopey pigeons were waiting until
the water and grass had chewed up the bread for them, so
they wouldn't have to do it themselves.

I let the baby play in the sandbox and I sat down on a bench
and looked around. There was a beatnik sitting at the other
end of the bench. He had his sleeping bag beside him and he
was eating apple turnovers. He had a huge sack of apple turnovers and he was gobbling them down like a turkey. It was
probably a more valid protest than picketing missile bases.

The baby played in the sandbox. She had on a red dress
and the Catholic church was towering up behind her red dress.
There was a brick john between her dress and the church. It
was there by no accident. Ladies to the left and gents to the
right.

A red dress, I thought. Wasn't the woman who set John
Dillinger up for the FBI wearing a red dress? They called
her "The Woman in Red."

It seemed to me that was right. It was a red dress, but so
far, John Dillinger was nowhere in sight. My daughter
played alone in the sandbox.

Sandbox minus John Dillinger equals what?

The beatnik went and got a drink of water from the fountain
that was crucified on the wall of the brick john, more toward
the gents than the ladies. He had to wash all those apple turnovers down his throat.

There were three sprinklers going in the park. There was one in front of the Benjamin Franklin statue and one to the side of him and one just behind him. They were all turning in circles. I saw Benjamin Franklin standing there patiently through the water.

The sprinkler to the side of Benjamin Franklin hit the left-hand tree. It sprayed hard against the trunk and knocked some leaves down from the tree, and then it hit the center tree, sprayed hard against the trunk and more leaves fell. Then it sprayed against Benjamin Franklin, the water shot out to the sides of the stone and a mist drifted down off the water. Benjamin Franklin got his feet wet.

The sun was shining down hard on me. The sun was bright and hot. After a while the sun made me think of my own discomfort. The only shade fell on the beatnik.

The shade came down off the Lillie Hitchcock Coit statue of some metal fireman saving a metal broad from a _mental_ fire. The beatnik now lay on the bench and the shade was two feet longer than he was.

A friend of mine has written a poem about that statue. Goddamn, I wish he would write another poem about that statue, so it would give me some shade two feet longer than my body.

I was right about "The Woman in Red," because ten minutes — later they blasted John Dillinger down in the sandbox. The sound of the machine-gun fire startled the pigeons and they hurried on into the church.

My daughter was seen leaving in a huge black car shortly after that. She couldn't talk yet, but that didn't make any difference. The red dress did it all.

John Dillinger's body lay half in and half out of the sandbox, more toward the ladies than the gents. He was leaking blood like those capsules we used to use with oleomargarine, in those good old days when oleo was white like lard.

The huge black car pulled out and went up the street, batlight shining off the top. It stopped in front of the ice-cream parlor at Filbert and Stockton.

An agent got out and went in and bought two hundred double-decker ice-cream cones. He needed a wheelbarrow to get them back to the car.

THE LAST TIME I SAW
TROUT FISHING IN AMERICA

The last time we met was in July on the Big Wood River, ten
miles away from Ketchum. It was just after Hemingway had
killed himself there, but I didn't know about his death at the
time. I didn't know about it until I got back to San Francisco
weeks after the thing had happened and picked up a copy of
Life magazine. There was a photograph of Hemingway on the
cover.

"I wonder what Hemingway's up to," I said to myself. I
looked inside the magazine and turned the pages to his death.
Trout Fishing in America forgot to tell me about it. I'm certain he knew. It must have slipped his mind.

The woman who travels with me had menstrual cramps.
She wanted to rest for a while, so I took the baby and my spin-
ning rod and went down to the Big Wood River. That's where
I met Trout Fishing in America.

I was casting a Super-Duper out into the river and letting
it swing down with the current and then ride on the water up
close to the shore. It fluttered there slowly and Trout Fishing in America watched the baby while we talked.

I remember that he gave her some colored rocks to play
with. She liked him and climbed up onto his lap and she started putting the rocks in his shirt pocket.

We talked about Great Falls, Montana. I told Trout Fishing in America about a winter I spent as a child in Great Falls.
"It was during the war and I saw a Deanna Durbin movie seven
times," I said.

The baby put a blue rock in Trout Fishing in America's
shirt pocket and he said, "I've been to Great Falls many
times. I remember Indians and fur traders. I remember
Lewis and Clark, but I don't remember ever seeing a Deanna
Durbin movie in Great Falls."

"I know what you mean," I said. "The other people in Great Falls did not share my enthusiasm for Deanna Durbin. The theater was always empty. There was a darkness to that theater different from any theater I've been in since. Maybe it was the snow outside and Deanna Durbin inside. I don't know what it was."

"What was the name of the movie?" Trout Fishing in America said.

"I don't know," I said. "She sang a lot. Maybe she was a chorus girl who wanted to go to college or she was a rich girl or they needed money for something or she did something. Whatever it was about, she sang! and sang! but I can't remember a God-damn word of it.

"One afternoon after I had seen the Deanna Durbin movie again, I went down to the Missouri River. Part of the Missouri was frozen over. There was a railroad bridge there. I was very relieved to see that the Missouri River had not changed and begun to look like Deanna Durbin.

"I'd had a childhood fancy that I would walk down to the Missouri River and it would look just like a Deanna Durbin movie—a chorus girl who wanted to go to college or she was a rich girl or they needed money for something or she did something.

"To this day I don't know why I saw that movie seven times. It was just as deadly as The Cabinet of Doctor Caligari. I wonder if the Missouri River is still there?" I said.

"It is," Trout Fishing in America said smiling. "But it doesn't look like Deanna Durbin."

The baby by this time had put a dozen or so of the colored rocks in Trout Fishing in America's shirt pocket. He looked at me and smiled and waited for me to go on about Great Falls, but just then I had a fair strike on my Super-Duper. I jerked the rod back and missed the fish.

Trout Fishing in America said, "I know that fish who just struck. You'll never catch him."

"Oh," I said.

"Forgive me," Trout Fishing in America said. "Go on ahead and try for him. He'll hit a couple of times more, but you won't catch him. He's not a particularly smart fish. Just lucky. Sometimes that's all you need."

"Yeah," I said. "You're right there."

I cast out again and continued talking about Great Falls.

90

Then in correct order I recited the twelve least important things ever said about Great Falls, Montana. For the twelfth and least important thing of all, I said, "Yeah, the telephone would ring in the morning. I'd get out of bed. I didn't have to answer the telephone. That had all been taken care of, years in advance.

"It would still be dark outside and the yellow wallpaper in the hotel room would be running back off the light bulb. I'd put my clothes on and go down to the restaurant where my stepfather cooked all night.

"I'd have breakfast, hot cakes, eggs and whatnot. Then he'd make my lunch for me and it would always be the same thing: a piece of pie and a stone-cold pork sandwich. Afterwards I'd walk to school. I mean the three of us, the Holy Trinity: me, a piece of pie, and a stone-cold pork sandwich. This went on for months.

"Fortunately it stopped one day without my having to do anything serious like grow up. We packed our stuff and left town on a bus. That was Great Falls, Montana. You say the Missouri River is still there?"

"Yes, but it doesn't look like Deanna Durbin," Trout Fishing in America said. "I remember the day Lewis discovered the falls. They left their camp at sunrise and a few hours later they came upon a beautiful plain and on the plain were more buffalo than they had ever seen before in one place.

"They kept on going until they heard the faraway sound of a waterfall and saw a distant column of spray rising and disappearing. They followed the sound as it got louder and louder. After a while the sound was tremendous and they were at the great falls of the Missouri River. It was about noon when they got there.

"A nice thing happened that afternoon, they went fishing below the falls and caught half a dozen trout, good ones, too, from sixteen to twenty-three inches long.

"That was June 13, 1805.

"No, I don't think Lewis would have understood it if the Missouri River had suddenly begun to look like a Deanna Durbin movie, like a chorus girl who wanted to go to college," Trout Fishing in America said.

91

IN THE CALIFORNIA BUSH

I've come home from Trout Fishing in America, the highway
bent its long smooth anchor about my neck and then stopped.
Now I live in this place. It took my whole life to get here, to
get to this strange cabin above Mill Valley.

We're staying with Pard and his girlfriend. They have
rented a cabin for three months, June 15th to September 15th,
for a hundred dollars. We are a funny bunch, all living here
together.

Pard was born of Okie parents in British Nigeria and came
to America when he was two years old and was raised as a
ranch kid in Oregon, Washington and Idaho.

He was a machine-gunner in the Second World War, against
the Germans. He fought in France and Germany. Sergeant
Pard. Then he came back from the war and went to some
hick college in Idaho.

After he graduated from college, he went to Paris and became an Existentialist. He had a photograph taken of Exis-
tentialism and himself sitting at a sidewalk cafe. Pard was
wearing a beard and he looked as if he had a huge soul, with
barely enough room in his body to contain it.

When Pard came back to America from Paris, he worked
as a tugboat man on San Francisco Bay and as a railroad
man in the roundhouse at Filer, Idaho.

Of course, during this time he got married and had a kid.
The wife and kid are gone now, blown away like apples by the
fickle wind of the Twentieth Century. I guess the fickle wind
of all time. The family that fell in the autumn.

After he split up with his wife, he went to Arizona and was
a reporter and editor of newspapers. He honky-tonked in
Naco, a Mexican border town, drank Mescal Triunfo, played
cards and shot the roof of his house full of bullet holes.

Pard tells a story about waking one morning in Naco, all hungover, with the whips and jingles. A friend of his was sitting at the table with a bottle of whisky beside him.

Pard reached over and picked up a gun off a chair and took aim at the whisky bottle and fired. His friend was then sitting there, covered with flecks of glass, blood and whisky. "What the fuck you do that for?" he said.

Now in his late thirties Pard works at a print shop for $1.35 an hour. It is an avant-garde print shop. They print poetry and experimental prose. They pay him $1.35 an hour for operating a linotype machine. A $1.35 linotype operator is hard to find, outside of Hong Kong or Albania.

Sometimes when he goes down there, they don't even have enough lead for him. They buy their lead like soap, a bar or two at a time.

Pard's girlfriend is a Jew. Twenty-four years old, getting over a bad case of hepatitis, she kids Pard about a nude photograph of her that has the possibility of appearing in Playboy magazine.

"There's nothing to worry about," she says. "If they use that photograph, it only means that 12,000,000 men will look at my boobs."

This is all very funny to her. Her parents have money. As she sits in the other room in the California bush, she's on her father's payroll in New York.

What we eat is funny and what we drink is even more hilarious: turkeys, Gallo port, hot dogs, watermelons, Popeyes, salmon croquettes, frappes, Christian Brothers port, orange rye bread, canteloupes, Popeyes, salads, cheese—booze, grub and Popeyes.

Popeyes?

We read books like The Thief's Journal, Set This House on Fire, The Naked Lunch, Krafft-Ebing. We read Krafft-Ebing aloud all the time as if he were Kraft dinner.

"The mayor of a small town in Eastern Portugal was seen one morning pushing a wheelbarrow full of sex organs into the city hall. He was of tainted family. He had a woman's shoe in his back pocket. It had been there all night." Things like this make us laugh.

The woman who owns this cabin will come back in the autumn. She's spending the summer in Europe. When she comes back, she will spend only one day a week out here: Saturday.

She will never spend the night because she's afraid to. There is something here that makes her afraid.

Pard and his girlfriend sleep in the cabin and the baby sleeps in the basement, and we sleep outside, under the apple tree, waking at dawn to stare out across San Francisco Bay and then we go back to sleep again and wake once more, this time for a very strange thing to happen, and then we go back to sleep again after it has happened, and wake at sunrise to stare out across the bay.

Afterwards we go back to sleep again and the sun rises steadily hour after hour, staying in the branches of a eucalyptus tree just a ways down the hill, keeping us cool and asleep and in the shade. At last the sun pours over the top of the tree and then we have to get up, the hot sun upon us.

We go into the house and begin that two-hour yak-yak activity we call breakfast. We sit around and bring ourselves slowly back to consciousness, treating ourselves like fine pieces of china, and after we finish the last cup of the last cup of the last cup of coffee, it's time to think about lunch or go to the Goodwill in Fairfax.

So here we are, living in the California bush above Mill Valley. We could look right down on the main street of Mill Valley if it were not for the eucalyptus tree. We have to park the car a hundred yards away and come here along a tunnel-like path.

If all the Germans Pard killed during the war with his machine-gun were to come and stand in their uniforms around this place, it would make us pretty nervous.

There's the warm sweet smell of blackberry bushes along the path and in the late afternoon, quail gather around a dead unrequited tree that has fallen bridelike across the path. Sometimes I go down there and jump the quail. I just go down there to get them up off their butts. They're such beautiful birds. They set their wings and sail on down the hill.

O he was the one who was born to be king! That one, turning down through the Scotch broom and going over an upside-down car abandoned in the yellow grass. That one, his gray wings.

One morning last week, part way through the dawn, I awoke under the apple tree, to hear a dog barking and the rapid sound of hoofs coming toward me. The millennium? An invasion of Russians all wearing deer feet?

94

I opened my eyes and saw a deer running straight at me. It was a buck with large horns. There was a police dog chasing after it.

Arfwowfuck! Noisepoundpoundpoundpoundpoundpound! POUND! POUND!

The deer didn't swerve away. He just kept running straight at me, long after he had seen me, a second or two had passed.

Arfwowfuck! Noisepoundpoundpoundpoundpoundpound! POUND! POUND!

I could have reached out and touched him when he went by.

He ran around the house, circling the john, with the dog hot after him. They vanished over the hillside, leaving streamers of toilet paper behind them, flowing out and entangled through the bushes and vines.

Then along came the doe. She started up the same way, but not moving as fast. Maybe she had strawberries in her head.

"Whoa!" I shouted. "Enough is enough! I'm not selling newspapers!"

The doe stopped in her tracks, twenty-five feet away and turned and went down around the eucalyptus tree.

Well, that's how it's gone now for days and days. I wake up just before they come. I wake up for them in the same manner as I do for the dawn and the sunrise. Suddenly knowing they're on their way.

THE LAST MENTION OF TROUT
FISHING IN AMERICA SHORTY

Saturday was the first day of autumn and there was a festival
being held at the church of Saint Francis. It was a hot day
and the Ferris wheel was turning in the air like a thermo-
meter bent in a circle and given the grace of music.

But all this goes back to another time, to when my daughter was conceived. We'd just moved into a new apartment and
the lights hadn't been turned on yet. We were surrounded by
unpacked boxes of stuff and there was a candle burning like
milk on a saucer. So we got one in and we're sure it was the
right one.

A friend was sleeping in another room. In retrospect I
hope we didn't wake him up, though he has been awakened and
gone to sleep hundreds of times since then.

During the pregnancy I stared innocently at that growing
human center and had no idea the child therein contained
would ever meet Trout Fishing in America Shorty.

Saturday afternoon we went down to Washington Square.
We put the baby down on the grass and she took off running
toward Trout Fishing in America Shorty who was sitting under the trees by the Benjamin Franklin statue.

He was on the ground leaning up against the right-hand
tree. There were some garlic sausages and some bread sitting in his wheelchair as if it were a display counter in a
strange grocery store.

The baby ran down there and tried to make off with one of
his sausages.

Trout Fishing in America Shorty was instantly alerted,
then he saw it was a baby and relaxed. He tried to coax her
to come over and sit on his legless lap. She hid behind his
wheelchair, staring past the metal at him, one of her hands
holding onto a wheel.

"Come here, kid," he said. "Come over and see old Trout
Fishing in America Shorty."

Just then the Benjamin Franklin statue turned green like
a traffic light, and the baby noticed the sandbox at the other
end of the park.

The sandbox suddenly looked better to her than Trout Fishing in America Shorty. She didn't care about his sausages
any more either.

She decided to take advantage of the green light, and she
crossed over to the sandbox.

Trout Fishing in America Shorty stared after her as if
the space between them were a river growing larger and
larger.

WITNESS FOR TROUT FISHING

IN AMERICA PEACE

In San Francisco around Easter time last year, they had a trout fishing in America peace parade. They had thousands of red stickers printed and they pasted them on their small foreign cars, and on means of national communication like telephone poles.

The stickers had WITNESS FOR TROUT FISHING IN AMERICA PEACE printed on them.

Then this group of college- and high-school-trained Communists, along with some Communist clergymen and their Marxist-taught children, marched to San Francisco from Sunnyvale, a Communist nerve center about forty miles away.

It took them four days to walk to San Francisco. They stopped overnight at various towns along the way, and slept on the lawns of fellow travelers.

They carried with them Communist trout fishing in America peace propaganda posters:

"DON'T DROP AN H-BOMB ON THE OLD FISHING HOLE!"

"ISAAC WALTON WOULD'VE HATED THE BOMB!"

"ROYAL COACHMAN, SI! ICBM, NO!"

They carried with them many other trout fishing in America peace inducements, all following the Communist world conquest line: the Gandhian nonviolence Trojan horse.

When these young, hard-core brainwashed members of the Communist conspiracy reached the "Panhandle," the emigre Oklahoma Communist sector of San Francisco, thousands of other Communists were waiting for them. These were Communists who couldn't walk very far. They barely had enough strength to make it downtown.

Thousands of Communists, protected by the police, marched

down to Union Square, located in the very heart of San Francisco. The Communist City Hall riots in 1960 had presented evidence of it, the police let hundreds of Communists escape, but the trout fishing in America peace parade was the final indictment: police protection.

Thousands of Communists marched right into the heart of San Francisco, and Communist speakers incited them for hours and the young people wanted to blow up Coit Tower, but the Communist clergy told them to put away their plastic bombs.

"Therefore all things whatsoever ye would that men should do to you, do ye even so to them . . . There will be no need for explosives," they said.

America needs no other proof. The Red shadow of the Gandhian nonviolence Trojan horse has fallen across America, and San Francisco is its stable.

Obsolete is the mad rapist's legendary piece of candy. At this very moment, Communist agents are handing out Witness for trout fishing in America peace tracts to innocent children riding the cable cars.

FOOTNOTE CHAPTER TO

"RED LIP"

Living in the California bush we had no garbage service. Our
garbage was never greeted in the early morning by a man
with a big smile on his face and a kind word or two. We
couldn't burn any of the garbage because it was the dry seas-
on and everything was ready to catch on fire anyway, including ourselves. The garbage was a problem for a little while
and then we discovered a way to get rid of it.

We took the garbage down to where there were three abandoned houses in a row. We carried sacks full of tin cans,
papers, peelings, bottles and Popeyes.

We stopped at the last abandoned house where there were
thousands of old receipts to the San Francisco <u>Chronicle</u>
thrown all over the bed and the children's toothbrushes were
still in the bathroom medicine cabinet.

Behind the place was an old outhouse and to get down to it,
you had to follow the path down past some apple trees and a
patch of strange plants that we thought were either a good
spice that would certainly enhance our cooking or the plants
were deadly nightshade that would cause our cooking to be
less.

We carried the garbage down to the outhouse and always
opened the door slowly because that was the only way you
could open it, and on the wall there was a roll of toilet paper,
so old it looked like a relative, perhaps a cousin, to the Mag-
na Carta.

We lifted up the lid of the toilet and dropped the garbage
down into the darkness. This went on for weeks and weeks
until it became very funny to lift the lid of the toilet and instead of seeing darkness below or maybe the murky abstract
outline of garbage, we saw bright, definite and lusty garbage
heaped up almost to the top.

If you were a stranger and went down there to take an innocent crap, you would've had quite a surprise when you lifted up the lid.

We left the California bush just before it became necessary to stand on the toilet seat and step into that hole, crushing the garbage down like an accordion into the abyss.

THE CLEVELAND WRECKING

YARD

Until recently my knowledge about the Cleveland Wrecking
Yard had come from a couple of friends who'd bought things
there. One of them bought a huge window: the frame, glass
and everything for just a few dollars. It was a fine-looking
window.

Then he chopped a hole in the side of his house up on
Potrero Hill and put the window in. Now he has a panoramic
view of the San Francisco County Hospital.

He can practically look right down into the wards and see
old magazines eroded like the Grand Canyon from endless
readings. He can practically hear the patients thinking about
breakfast: I hate milk, and thinking about dinner: I hate peas,
and then he can watch the hospital slowly drown at night,
hopelessly entangled in huge bunches of brick seaweed.

He bought that window at the Cleveland Wrecking Yard.

My other friend bought an iron roof at the Cleveland Wrecking Yard and took the roof down to Big Sur in an old station
wagon and then he carried the iron roof on his back up the
side of a mountain. He carried up half the roof on his back.
It was no picnic. Then he bought a mule, George, from Pleasanton. George carried up the other half of the roof.

The mule didn't like what was happening at all. He lost a
lot of weight because of the ticks, and the smell of the wild-
cats up on the plateau made him too nervous to graze there.
My friend said jokingly that George had lost around two hundred pounds. The good wine country around Pleasanton in the
Livermore Valley probably had looked a lot better to George
than the wild side of the Santa Lucia Mountains.

My friend's place was a shack right beside a huge fireplace where there had once been a great mansion during the
1920s, built by a famous movie actor. The mansion was built

before there was even a road down at Big Sur. The mansion had been brought over the mountains on the backs of mules, strung out like ants, bringing visions of the good life to the poison oak, the ticks, and the salmon.

The mansion was on a promontory, high over the Pacific. Money could see farther in the 1920s, and one could look out and see whales and the Hawaiian Islands and the Kuomintang in China.

The mansion burned down years ago.

The actor died.

His mules were made into soap.

His mistresses became bird nests of wrinkles.

Now only the fireplace remains as a sort of Carthaginian homage to Hollywood.

I was down there a few weeks ago to see my friend's roof. I wouldn't have passed up the chance for a million dollars, as they say. The roof looked like a colander to me. If that roof and the rain were running against each other at Bay Meadows, I'd bet on the rain and plan to spend my winnings at the World's Fair in Seattle.

My own experience with the Cleveland Wrecking Yard began two days ago when I heard about a used trout stream they had on sale out at the Yard. So I caught the Number 15 bus on Columbus Avenue and went out there for the first time.

There were two Negro boys sitting behind me on the bus. They were talking about Chubby Checker and the Twist. They thought that Chubby Checker was only fifteen years old because he didn't have a mustache. Then they talked about some other guy who did the twist forty-four hours in a row until he saw George Washington crossing the Delaware.

"Man, that's what I call twisting," one of the kids said.

"I don't think I could twist no forty-four hours in a row," the other kid said. "That's a lot of twisting."

I got off the bus right next to an abandoned Time Gasoline filling station and an abandoned fifty-cent self-service car wash. There was a long field on one side of the filling station. The field had once been covered with a housing project during the war, put there for the shipyard workers.

On the other side of the Time filling station was the Cleveland Wrecking Yard. I walked down there to have a look at the used trout stream. The Cleveland Wrecking Yard has a very long front window filled with signs and merchandise.

There was a sign in the window advertising a laundry marking machine for $65.00. The original cost of the machine was $175.00. Quite a saving.

There was another sign advertising new and used two and three ton hoists. I wondered how many hoists it would take to move a trout stream.

There was another sign that said:

THE FAMILY GIFT CENTER,
GIFT SUGGESTIONS FOR THE ENTIRE FAMILY

The window was filled with hundreds of items for the entire family. Daddy, do you know what I want for Christmas? What, son? A bathroom. Mommy, do you know what I want for Christmas? What, Patricia? Some roofing material.

There were jungle hammocks in the window for distant relatives and dollar-ten-cent gallons of earth-brown enamel paint for other loved ones.

There was also a big sign that said:

USED TROUT STREAM FOR SALE.
MUST BE SEEN TO BE APPRECIATED.

I went inside and looked at some ship's lanterns that were for sale next to the door. Then a salesman came up to me and said in a pleasant voice, "Can I help you?"

"Yes," I said. "I'm curious about the trout stream you have for sale. Can you tell me something about it? How are you selling it?"

"We're selling it by the foot length. You can buy as little as you want or you can buy all we've got left. A man came in here this morning and bought 563 feet. He's going to give it to his niece for a birthday present," the salesman said.

"We're selling the waterfalls separately of course, and the trees and birds, flowers, grass and ferns we're also selling extra. The insects we're giving away free with a minimum purchase of ten feet of stream."

"How much are you selling the stream for?" I asked.

"Six dollars and fifty-cents a foot," he said. "That's for the first hundred feet. After that it's five dollars a foot."

"How much are the birds?" I asked.

"Thirty-five cents apiece," he said. "But of course they're used. We can't guarantee anything."

"How wide is the stream?" I asked. "You said you were

104

selling it by the length, didn't you?"

"Yes," he said. "We're selling it by the length. Its width runs between five and eleven feet. You don't have to pay anything extra for width. It's not a big stream, but it's very pleasant."

"What kinds of animals do you have?" I asked.

"We only have three deer left," he said.

"Oh . . . What about flowers?"

"By the dozen," he said.

"Is the stream clear?" I asked.

"Sir," the salesman said. "I wouldn't want you to think that we would ever sell a murky trout stream here. We always make sure they're running crystal clear before we even think about moving them."

"Where did the stream come from?" I asked.

"Colorado," he said. "We moved it with loving care. We've never damaged a trout stream yet. We treat them all as if they were china."

"You're probably asked this all the time, but how's fishing in the stream?" I asked.

"Very good," he said. "Mostly German browns, but there are a few rainbows."

"What do the trout cost?" I asked.

"They come with the stream," he said. "Of course it's all luck. You never know how many you're going to get or how big they are. But the fishing's very good, you might say it's excellent. Both bait and dry fly," he said smiling.

"Where's the stream at?" I asked. "I'd like to take a look at it."

"It's around in back," he said. "You go straight through that door and then turn right until you're outside. It's stacked in lengths. You can't miss it. The waterfalls are upstairs in the used plumbing department."

"What about the animals?"

"Well, what's left of the animals are straight back from the stream. You'll see a bunch of our trucks parked on a road by the railroad tracks. Turn right on the road and follow it down past the piles of lumber. The animal shed's right at the end of the lot."

"Thanks," I said. "I think I'll look at the waterfalls first. You don't have to come with me. Just tell me how to get there and I'll find my own way."

105

"All right," he said. "Go up those stairs. You'll see a bunch of doors and windows, turn left and you'll find the used plumbing department. Here's my card if you need any help."

"Okay," I said. "You've been a great help already. Thanks a lot. I'll take a look around."

"Good luck," he said.

I went upstairs and there were thousands of doors there. I'd never seen so many doors before in my life. You could have built an entire city out of those doors. Doorstown. And there were enough windows up there to build a little suburb entirely out of windows. Windowville.

I turned left and went back and saw the faint glow of pearl-colored light. The light got stronger and stronger as I went farther back, and then I was in the used plumbing department, surrounded by hundreds of toilets.

The toilets were stacked on shelves. They were stacked five toilets high. There was a skylight above the toilets that made them glow like the Great Taboo Pearl of the South Sea movies.

Stacked over against the wall were the waterfalls. There were about a dozen of them, ranging from a drop of a few feet to a drop of ten or fifteen feet.

There was one waterfall that was over sixty feet long. There were tags on the pieces of the big falls describing the correct order for putting the falls back together again.

The waterfalls all had price tags on them. They were more expensive than the stream. The waterfalls were selling for $19.00 a foot.

I went into another room where there were piles of sweet-smelling lumber, glowing a soft yellow from a different color skylight above the lumber. In the shadows at the edge of the room under the sloping roof of the building were many sinks and urinals covered with dust, and there was also another waterfall about seventeen feet long, lying there in two lengths and already beginning to gather dust.

I had seen all I wanted of the waterfalls, and now I was very curious about the trout stream, so I followed the salesman's directions and ended up outside the building.

O I had never in my life seen anything like that trout stream. It was stacked in piles of various lengths: ten, fifteen, twenty feet, etc. There was one pile of hundred-foot

106

lengths. There was also a box of scraps. The scraps were in odd sizes ranging from six inches to a couple of feet.

There was a loudspeaker on the side of the building and soft music was coming out. It was a cloudy day and seagulls were circling high overhead.

Behind the stream were big bundles of trees and bushes. They were covered with sheets of patched canvas. You could see the tops and roots sticking out the ends of the bundles.

I went up close and looked at the lengths of stream. I could see some trout in them. I saw one good fish. I saw some crawdads crawling around the rocks at the bottom.

It looked like a fine stream. I put my hand in the water. It was cold and felt good.

I decided to go around to the side and look at the animals. I saw where the trucks were parked beside the railroad tracks. I followed the road down past the piles of lumber, back to the shed where the animals were.

The salesman had been right. They were practically out of animals. About the only thing they had left in any abundance were mice. There were hundreds of mice.

Beside the shed was a huge wire birdcage, maybe fifty feet high, filled with many kinds of birds. The top of the cage had a piece of canvas over it, so the birds wouldn't get wet when it rained. There were woodpeckers and wild canaries and sparrows.

On my way back to where the trout stream was piled, I found the insects. They were inside a prefabricated steel building that was selling for eighty-cents a square foot. There was a sign over the door. It said

INSECTS

A HALF-SUNDAY HOMAGE TO A
WHOLE LEONARDO DA VINCI

On this funky winter day in rainy San Francisco I've had a vision of Leonardo da Vinci. My woman's out slaving away, no day off, working on Sunday. She left here at eight o'clock this morning for Powell and California. I've been sitting here ever since like a toad on a log dreaming about Leonardo da Vinci.

I dreamt he was on the South Bend Tackle Company payroll, but of course, he was wearing different clothes and speaking with a different accent and possessor of a different childhood, perhaps an American childhood spent in a town like Lordsburg, New Mexico, or Winchester, Virginia.

I saw him inventing a new spinning lure for trout fishing in America. I saw him first of all working with his imagination, then with metal and color and hooks, trying a little of this and a little of that, and then adding motion and then taking it away and then coming back again with a different motion, and in the end the lure was invented.

He called his bosses in. They looked at the lure and all fainted. Alone, standing over their bodies, he held the lure in his hand and gave it a name. He called it "The Last Supper." Then he went about waking up his bosses.

In a matter of months that trout fishing lure was the sensation of the twentieth century, far outstripping such shallow accomplishments as Hiroshima or Mahatma Gandhi. Millions of "The Last Supper" were sold in America. The Vatican ordered ten thousand and they didn't even have any trout there.

Testimonials poured in. Thirty-four ex-presidents of the United States all said, "I caught my limit on 'The Last Supper.'"

TROUT FISHING IN AMERICA

NIB

He went up to Chemault, that's in Eastern Oregon, to cut
Christmas trees. He was working for a very small enter-
prise. He cut the trees, did the cooking and slept on the
kitchen floor. It was cold and there was snow on the ground.
The floor was hard. Somewhere along the line, he found an
old Air Force flight jacket. That was a big help in the cold.

The only woman he could find up there was a three-hundred-
pound Indian squaw. She had twin fifteen-year-old daughters
and he wanted to get into them. But the squaw worked it so
he only got into her. She was clever that way.

The people he was working for wouldn't pay him up there.
They said he'd get it all in one sum when they got back to
San Francisco. He'd taken the job because he was broke,
really broke.

He waited and cut trees in the snow, laid the squaw,
cooked bad food—they were on a tight budget—and he
washed the dishes. Afterwards, he slept on the kitchen floor
in his Air Force flight jacket.

When they finally got back to town with the trees, those
guys didn't have any money to pay him off. He had to wait
around the lot in Oakland until they sold enough trees to pay
him off.

"Here's a lovely tree, ma'am."

"How much?"

"Ten dollars."

"That's too much."

"I have a lovely two-dollar tree here, ma'am. Actually,
it's only half a tree, but you can stand it up right next to a
wall and it'll look great, ma'am."

"I'll take it. I can put it right next to my weather clock.
This tree is the same color as the queen's dress. I'll take it.

109

You said two dollars?"

"That's right, ma'am."

"Hello, sir. Yes . . . Uh-huh . . . Yes . . . You say
that you want to bury your aunt with a Christmas tree in her
coffin? Uh-huh . . . She wanted it that way . . . I'll see
what I can do for you, sir. Oh, you have the measurements
of the coffin with you? Very good . . . We have our coffin-
sized Christmas trees right over here, sir."

Finally he was paid off and he came over to San Francisco and had a good meal, a steak dinner at Le Boeuf and some
good booze, Jack Daniels, and then went out to the Fillmore
and picked up a good-looking, young, Negro whore, and he
got laid in the Albert Bacon Fall Hotel.

The next day he went down to a fancy stationery store on
Market Street and bought himself a thirty-dollar fountain pen,
one with a gold nib.

He showed it to me and said, "Write with this, but don't
write hard because this pen has got a gold nib, and a gold
nib is very impressionable. After a while it takes on the per-
sonality of the writer. Nobody else can write with it. This
pen becomes just like a person's shadow. It's the only pen
to have. But be careful."

I thought to myself what a lovely nib trout fishing in America would make with a stroke of cool green trees along the
river's shore, wild flowers and dark fins pressed against
the paper.

PRELUDE TO THE
MAYONNAISE CHAPTER

"The Eskimos live among ice all their lives but have no single word for ice." —Man: His First Million Years, by M. F. Ashley Montagu

"Human language is in some ways similar to, but in other ways vastly different from, other kinds of animal communication. We simply have no idea about its evolutionary history, though many people have speculated about its possible origins. There is, for instance, the 'bow-bow' theory, that language started from attempts to imitate animal sounds. Or the 'ding-dong' theory, that it arose from natural sound-producing responses. Or the 'pooh-pooh' theory, that it began with violent outcries and exclamations . . . We have no way of knowing whether the kinds of men represented by the earliest fossils could talk or not . . . Language does not leave fossils, at least not until it has become written . . ." —Man in Nature, by Marston Bates

"But no animal up a tree can initiate a culture." —"The Simian Basis of Human Mechanics," in Twilight of Man, by Earnest Albert Hooton

Expressing a human need, I always wanted to write a book that ended with the word Mayonnaise.

THE MAYONNAISE CHAPTER

Feb 3-1952

Dearest Florence and Harv.

    I just heard from Edith about
the passing of Mr. Good. Our heart
goes out to you in deepest sympathy
Gods will be done. He has lived a
good long life and he has gone to
a better place. You were expecting
it and it was nice you could see
him yesterday even if he did not
know you. You have our prayers
and love and we will see you soon.
    God bless you both.

Love Mother and Nancy.

P.S.
Sorry I forgot to give you the mayonaise.